The Book Lady

Janet West and Laura Stebbing operated the mobile library that travelled the villages of north-east Essex on a schedule as precise as a railway timetable. When Janet's body was found at a lonely spot on the bank of the River Colne, Chief Inspector Millson wondered why anyone would murder such a respectable and well-liked woman. And where was she going at night by the river? Surely she hadn't been alone?

There was no obvious suspect and as his investigation proceeded he discovered there was more to the friendly librarian than he realized. Then Laura took part in a reconstruction of Janet's movements on the night she was killed and suddenly there were three suspects.

In the end there were three murders too.

MALCOLM FORSYTHE

The Book Lady

THE CRIME CLUB
An Imprint of HarperCollins *Publishers*

First published in Great Britain in 1993
by The Crime Club, an imprint of
HarperCollins Publishers, 77–85 Fulham Palace Road,
Hammersmith, London W6 8JB

9 8 7 6 5 4 3 2 1

Malcolm Forsythe asserts the moral right to be identified
as the author of this work.

A catalogue record for this book is
available from the British Library.

ISBN 0 00 232481 4

Photoset in Linotron Baskerville by
Rowland Phototypesetting Ltd
Bury St Edmunds, Suffolk
Printed and bound in Great Britain by
HarperCollins Book Manufacturing, Glasgow.

CHAPTER 1

Jack Chappell found the body at six o'clock in the morning. It was barely an hour since dawn and the April morning was cold as his fishing boat sped upriver towards the quay at Tanniford on the last of the flood tide.

Huddled in the protective cuddy at the stern, Jack Chappell was comfortably warm in a thick woollen jersey and bib-fronted waterproof trousers. After a night's fishing in the North Sea he was looking forward to the breakfast of egg, bacon and fried bread his wife would have ready for him at his home in West Street.

In the well of the boat his crewman was sorting the night's catch into boxes. As soon as they berthed, the boxes of fish and shellfish would be transferred to Fred Hall's freezer sheds near the quay. From there the seafood would be despatched in white Suzuki vans to destinations all over East Anglia.

Jack Chappell eased the wheel and reduced speed to negotiate the bend in the Colne above Alresford Creek. Rounding the red channel buoy, he opened the throttle wide and the vessel surged forward, bow wave foaming against her dark blue hull, on the last stage of her journey.

Through the window of the cuddy he surveyed the familiar vista. Ahead of him, a tall building clad with corrugated sheeting marked Tanniford's small shipyard and the beginning of the village. Breaking the skyline beyond was the distinctive cupola on the tower of St Mary's church.

His gaze roamed the deserted banks either side . . . the empty fields . . . the rusting framework of disused Ballast Quay. Then something jarred his vision like a speck of dirt in the eye. His eyes swept the starboard bank again and spotted an alien splash of scarlet in the grass.

Holding the wheel with one hand, he stepped from behind the cuddy for a better view. The patch of colour was beside the path that ran along the riverbank from Alresford to Tanniford. With his free hand he reached for the binoculars on the shelf of the cuddy and put them to his eyes.

Lying on the ground was the body of a woman. What had caught his eye was the bright red of her underclothes against the green of the grass in the early morning light.

He put down the binoculars and stepped swiftly to the controls to throttle back the engine. As his crewman looked up from his work in surprise, he shouted to make himself heard above the thump of the diesel. 'Steve! There's a woman's body on the bank over there.'

The crewman came aft. 'Where?'

Jack Chappell pointed and handed him the binoculars. Steve Turner raised them to his eyes and refocused. 'Strewth! What'll us do?'

'I'll go ashore and have a look. You carry on up to the quay and I'll join you later.'

The other man nodded and took the wheel, holding the boat hove-to in midstream. Jack Chappell pulled on his thigh-length sea boots and clambered into the dinghy towing astern. Starting the outboard, he cast off and headed for the bank. Aboard the fishing boat Steve Turner opened the throttle, water creamed under the stern, and the vessel continued upriver.

Jack Chappell grounded the dinghy on the shallow slope of the riverbank. Jumping out, he dragged it from the water and scrambled up the wall of concrete blocks that had been built along the river after the East Coast floods in the 'fifties.

He reached the earth bank at the top and approached the body hesitantly. It wasn't the first time Jack Chappell had encountered a dead body—he'd pulled more than one from the sea in his time. Never a woman, though, and it disturbed him to see her sprawled indecently on her back, a black court shoe on one nyloned foot, the other foot shoeless.

There were brownish, blood-soaked strands among the blonde hairs of the head. Dropping to one knee he pressed a finger to the side of the woman's neck. There was no pulse.

A moment later he was hurrying along the riverbank to the shipyard office and a telephone.

Yesterday, Janet West had worked as usual. At half past eight she was picked up from her house near St Botolph's in Colchester by a yellow coach of the county mobile library service driven by her friend and colleague, Laura Stebbing.

Both women were in their early forties and wore navy-blue barathea skirts and white blouses. Physically, however, they were not at all alike. Janet was a natural blonde with a good figure that made her look younger than her forty-two years. Laura had mouse-coloured hair and was short and dumpy. The two had worked together for three years and the relationship between them was warm and harmonious.

Laura Stebbing reversed the rectangular-shaped coach out of the cul-de-sac where Janet lived and drove along Magdalen Street to the Hythe. As they waited in the queue of vehicles at the level-crossing, Janet opened her handbag and took out a small appointment diary.

Laura glanced sideways at her, smiling slyly. 'Busy day?'

'Fairly. Nothing before Great Bromley, though.'

The gates opened and Laura drove on and up the hill to the Colchester by-pass. Negotiating with difficulty three of the five mini-roundabouts that had now replaced the one large one, she headed east along the by-pass towards their first stop of the day at Burnt Heath.

Every week, from Tuesday to Friday, they set out on a different route each day, taking library facilities to villages in the north-east corner of the county. Monday was spent at the library headquarters in Colchester doing office work and gathering together the books that had been requested by readers during their rounds of the villages.

The coach was lined with shelves slanted upwards to prevent the five thousand or so books stacked along them from falling out as it travelled along the road. The book titles reflected the mix of borrowers who used the mobile library. Most of the readers were retired and elderly, but there were also pre-school children and their mothers and, in the school holidays, older children as well. The fiction comprised romances, westerns and crime novels and the non-fiction books covered subjects like handicrafts and leisure pursuits. Children's books were placed on the lower shelves where small children could reach them and there was a shelf of large print books for the near-sighted. In a cupboard behind the counter at the front end of the coach there was a sink, a chemical closet and a gas ring connected to a bottle of liquid gas.

Today, Wednesday, their route—as shown in the printed timetable issued to borrowers—would take them on a round trip through Burnt Heath, Great Bromley and other villages to Findlesham on the other side of the Colne.

In the small villages there was only one stop, but in larger villages the coach called at two and sometimes three different locations. The duration of the halts varied between fifteen minutes and an hour.

They reached their stop in Burnt Heath on schedule at nine o'clock. Laura Stebbing parked and there was a hiss of air as she pressed a button and the double doors opened in the centre of the coach. Easing her ample figure from the driving seat, she joined Janet at the counter. From a small wooden filing cabinet she drew out the box of reader's tickets for Burnt Heath and laid it on the counter.

An elderly, bald-headed man heaved himself up into the coach, wheezing heavily. Janet looked up and gave him a warm smile. 'Hullo, Ben.' Nimbly, her fingers searched the box for his reader's ticket.

'You got a nice book for me?' he asked. Watery eyes, the corneas blood-flecked, gazed hopefully at Janet.

She reached beneath the counter and brought out a book. 'You'll like this one,' she said, giving him a wink. 'I kept it specially.'

'Tah.' Lips peeled back from false teeth in a smile.

Extracting the title card from the pouch in the flyleaf, she inserted it into his reader's ticket, filed the ticket in the box and handed him the book.

He clutched it to his chest and tottered uncertainly to the door. Clinging to the handrail as though it were a lifeline, he lowered himself down the two steps to the ground.

'Poor old devil,' Laura said. 'Those books you get for him must be about his only pleasure in life.'

Promptly at nine-forty, Janet and Laura closed the library and drove to Great Bromley, arriving there at nine forty-five. The mobile library ran to a schedule as precise as a railway timetable.

At the village after Great Bromley, Janet took out her appointment diary as Laura parked beside the green. 'Andy Beddows wants his book changing today,' she said.

Taking a mirror from her handbag, she applied fresh lipstick and patted her hair into place. She selected a book from under the counter and descended from the coach, leaving Laura to deal with the borrowers.

She returned twenty minutes later smoking a cigarette and helped Laura file the tickets and sort the returned books away in the racks. Five minutes later they were on their way to the next stop.

They stopped for a lunch of sandwiches and coffee in a lay-by near Alresford and by three-thirty that afternoon their coach had reached Tanniford. Laura Stebbing drove on to the tarmac forecourt of the village hall next to the police station for their one-hour stop.

The coach soon filled with mothers and children on their way home from the school at Tanniford Cross, their push-

chairs and baby carriages left leaning against the side of
the coach. Inside, Janet and Laura stood at the counter
busily receiving returned books and date-stamping fresh
issues.

By four o'clock the rush was over. Janet West, with a
glance at her watch, opened a cupboard next to the counter
and lifted a weighty volume from the shelf. The title on it,
The Thousand and One Nights, was printed in gilt letters.

'Old Harry Smith?' Laura asked.

Janet nodded.

'Don't let him make us late this time,' Laura warned.

'I won't,' Janet promised.

Tucking the heavy book under her arm, she jumped
down from the coach and crossed the road into Queen
Street.

When she returned at half past four she was smiling
widely as she climbed up into the passenger seat. 'The old
rogue tried to date me for this evening,' she told Laura.
'Very persistent, he was.'

'What did you say?'

'I told him he was too young for that sort of thing.'

Laura Stebbing gave a hoot of laughter and started the
engine. She drove into the road and up the hill on the way
to their last stop of the day at Findlesham, on the other
side of the river from Tanniford.

In the bedroom of her terrace house that evening, Janet
West stripped off her clothes and padded across the landing
to the bathroom. She filled the bath and lay soaking con-
tentedly, periodically topping it up from the hot tap. Janet
loved her job and enjoyed every day of it, although she
found Mondays in the office a trifle boring.

After half an hour she clambered from the bath and dried
and powdered herself. Returning to the bedroom, she
dressed in the clothes and underwear she had laid out on
the bed. Then she went downstairs to the kitchen and pre-

pared and ate a light meal. At eight-thirty she left the house and got into her red Fiat Panda parked outside and drove off.

It was shortly before nine when she drove down the hill into Tanniford's short High Street and turned into East Street at the bottom. She could hear the clink of glasses and the murmur of voices from the Black Dog as she drove past into Spring Street. Dusk had fallen as she left home and it was fully dark when she turned on to the patch of waste ground in front of the shipyard and parked the car.

Stepping out, she locked the door and stood for a moment smoothing the wrinkles in her pleated skirt. Then she turned and headed for the entrance to the shipyard.

CHAPTER 2

Detective Chief Inspector George Millson arrived at the
murder scene just before seven. Most days since she had
returned to live with him, Millson ran his thirteen-year-old
daughter to school on his way to work. This morning when
he left, he'd laid a bristly cheek against hers as she lay
warm and sleepy in bed and told her to take the bus.

Driving along Colchester's Avenue of Remembrance, he
rubbed a hand over his cheeks and glanced at himself in
the car mirror. With his stubbled chin, short dark hair and
square jaw, he looked like a convict. He stretched across
to the glove compartment and took out a battery shaver.
There was hardly any traffic on the road and by the time
he reached the turning off the by-pass for Tanniford, he'd
successfully completed a one-handed shave.

The sun had risen but there was no warmth in the morning when he parked his blue Ford Sierra on the waste
ground in front of the shipyard. Several other vehicles were
parked there. Among them he recognized Scobie's Volks-
wagen Golf.

The morning shift had not yet arrived and the shipyard
was silent as he followed the public right of way across it
to the river. Tanniford's small, privately-owned yard built
coasting vessels and the keel of a three-thousand-ton ship
nearing completion rested on king-sized baulks of timber,
its stern overhanging the concrete slipway into the river.

On the far side of the yard Millson pushed open the
swinging iron gate on to the riverbank. He nodded to a
constable standing guard there and continued along the
path towards the cluster of figures a hundred yards further
along the bank.

It was a familiar scene to Millson and one that always

brought a quickening of the pulse and tightening of jaw muscles. The area had been taped-off and the police surgeon, photographer and scene of crime officer were at work on their tasks. Tall among another group of figures was the copper-coloured head of Detective-Sergeant Norris Scobie.

As Millson arrived, the police surgeon completed his preliminary examination and was meticulously arranging the body in its original position. He came to his feet and stood back to allow the photographer to take more pictures.

Millson grunted a greeting at no one in particular and ducked under the tape that had been staked out around the body. He stared morosely at the dead woman. She lay on her back, her lightweight fawn raincoat unbuttoned and open wide. He cast a professional eye over her, moving slowly from head to feet. He noted the shining blonde hair and the brown stains in it . . . the blue eyeshadow . . . mascara on the eyelashes . . . cosmetic blush on the cheeks . . . lightly carmined lips.

She was wearing a white, see-through blouse, a red bra showing beneath. The black pleated skirt was tidily in place over her legs and around the waist was a silver-buckled belt. She wore black tights or stockings and a black court shoe on one foot.

The eyes were closed and she looked peaceful. She could have been asleep, except for that patch of brownish-red in the blonde hair. Bending down for a closer examination, he was assailed by her cloying perfume. He straightened, his eyes scanning the ground around the body. The grass was still damp with dew and bore no signs of the body having been dragged over it.

He ducked out from under the tape and glanced questioningly at the police surgeon. 'How long?'

'From the rectal temperature I'd say she's been dead more than five hours—probably nearer ten. Death was most likely caused by blows to the head. Her underclothing is in place and it doesn't look as though she's been raped.'

The doctor snapped closed the clasp on his bag. 'That's all I can tell you. The rest is up to the pathologist.'

Millson turned to Scobie who had detached himself from the group and was standing beside him. 'Do we know who she is?'

'Janet West, according to the driving licence in her handbag. The bag was lying beside the body, but most of the contents are scattered around. The licence gives an address in Colchester and from the DVLC's date of birth code, she's aged forty-two.'

'Really?' Millson glanced back. 'She kept her age well.'

'We haven't found a notecase or any money, so presumably the motive was robbery.'

'Perhaps.' Millson shook his head doubtfully. 'This is a rural area. Handbag snatching is an urban crime. A handbag thief grabs the bag and runs, then pockets the cash and credit cards and dumps the bag. He doesn't drop it at the scene. And he doesn't kill ... not usually, anyway. Who found the body?'

'A fisherman. Name of Jack Chappell. He spotted her from his boat.' Scobie signalled to a man in yellow oilskin trousers and sea boots who was talking to a constable.

The man came forward and nodded to Millson. 'I were coming up river in me boat,' he said, 'when I see'd this bright red colour in the grass. Through the glasses I see'd a woman lying here so I come ashore and took a look. She were dead. She were the Book Lady,' he added.

Millson's eyes switched to the body on the ground. 'Did you move her or touch anything?'

'No, 'course not.'

'That was exactly how you found her?' Millson persisted, pointing to the body. 'Lying neatly, like she was taking a nap?'

Jack Chappell nodded.

'Then where's this red colour you say you saw?'

The man hesitated, looking confused. 'I . . . er . . . I did tidy her up a bit . . . pulled down her skirt—'

'You did *what*?' Millson growled.

'Well, it didn't seem right leaving her there with her legs an' all showing.'

Millson glared at him. 'What the hell did it matter? She was *dead*! The last thing I need is some thickhead like you interfering with the murder scene. Put her clothes back as you found them!'

Jack Chappell flushed angrily. He stepped under the tape and bent over Janet West's body. Self-consciously, he pulled up the skirt and a red satin waistslip beneath, to reveal matching French knickers above the stocking-tops.

Eyeing the colourful display, Millson was reminded of the lines of a Herrick poem he'd read in his youth. 'A sweet disorder in the dress kindles in clothes a wantonness'. And there was mention of 'a tempestuous petticoat' too, if he remembered correctly.

The fisherman stepped away, his face still more flushed. 'That's how she was.'

'Thank you,' Millson said heavily. He motioned to the hovering photographer. 'Take another picture.'

As the man focused his camera Millson stood behind him reappraising the scene. There were no bruises or scratch marks on the thighs and no signs of a struggle in the grass. She might not have resisted, of course—threatened with a knife, perhaps—but, like the doctor, he didn't think this was a case of rape.

He addressed Jack Chappell again. 'What time was it when you found her?'

'A bit after six o'clock.'

'Did you see anyone about?'

The fisherman shook his head.

'Is this path used much?'

'No, it don't lead anywhere . . . 'less you keeps walking

to Alresford. An' that's nigh on two miles. There's no cause for anyone to be about here early morning . . . 'less any of the shipyard workers in Alresford walk to work. An' that's not likely.' He gave a grunt. 'They's all got cars these days.'

'Thank you,' Millson said. 'No need to keep you any longer.'

Millson looked again at the body. The way a body lay often provided useful information. It puzzled him that Janet West was lying on her back. That was not how he would have expected her to lie after collapsing from fatal blows to the head. Nor could he work out how her skirt had rucked up high like that as she sank to the ground.

He raised his head and turned in a slow circle, surveying the river, the path along the bank and the open fields between the river and the nearest houses. He turned to Scobie.

'I wonder what she was doing here. It's a lonely spot.'

'Maybe taking a walk with a manfriend,' Scobie suggested. 'It was a mild spring evening.'

In the past he'd taken romantic strolls along this same riverbank with his girlfriend, Kathy Benson, who worked in the estate agent's in the High Street. Not lately, though. There was a coolness between them at the moment.

Millson sucked in his cheeks. 'A walk? Not in those high-heeled shoes. Oh, I think she was meeting someone all right. Not to go walking, though. Have you taken a note of the address on her licence?'

Scobie nodded. 'And I've got her doorkeys.'

'Right. Let's go and break the bad news.'

The undertakers arrived as they left. The scene of crime officer began supervising them to ensure they didn't destroy evidence as they removed the body. A plastic bag was put over the head to protect the head wounds and plastic bags tied over the hands to safeguard the taking of nail-parings later.

A collapsible trolley was unfolded and the corpse zipped

into a body-bag and lifted on to it. The trolley was wheeled along the path and through the shipyard to a plain black van waiting at the entrance.

CHAPTER 3

When Millson and Scobie pulled up outside Janet West's terrace house a coach was parked further along the street. It was buttercup yellow and had MOBILE LIBRARY in large letters across the rear and the county's coat of arms—three scimitars on a red field—emblazoned on the sides.

At the front door of Janet West's house a plump woman in a blue cardigan and blue skirt was alternately banging the knocker and peering through the letter-box. She turned as Millson and Scobie pushed open the garden gate.

'I can't get an answer,' she said helplessly.

'Are you a friend of Janet West?' Millson asked.

'Yes . . . I work with her.' She regarded Millson's bulky figure nervously. 'Who are you?'

'We're police officers. I'm Detective Chief Inspector Millson and this is Detective-Sergeant Scobie. And you are?'

'Mrs Stebbing. Laura Stebbing. Has something happened to Janet?'

'I'm afraid so. Does she live alone?'

'Yes.' She put a hand to her mouth. 'Oh God! Is she all right?'

'Why don't we go inside?' Millson suggested, motioning to Scobie. Scobie produced the bunch of keys and tried one in the lock.

'You've got her keys!' Laura Stebbing said accusingly. She took another look at Millson and backed away. 'Are you sure you're police officers?'

'Yes, madam.' Millson fished out his warrant card and held it out to her. 'Essex CID.'

She craned her neck forward and peered at the card suspiciously. Millson's photograph was a villainous likeness, but it seemed to reassure her and when Scobie opened the door and stood aside for her to enter she did so without demur.

In the hallway she allowed Scobie to take her elbow and steer her into the front room where she sank on to the settee of a three-piece suite. Millson and Scobie took an armchair each.

'I'm sorry to have to tell you that Janet West is dead, Mrs Stebbing,' Millson said.

'Oh no!' Laura Stebbing's face crumpled. 'What happened?'

'She was murdered.'

'*Murdered?*' Her lower lip started trembling. 'Oh God, how terrible. Where?'

Scobie answered. 'She was found on the riverbank at Tanniford early this morning,' he said. 'It looks as though she was robbed.'

'She always carried a lot of money in her bag. I warned her not to,' Laura Stebbing wailed.

'How well did you know her?' Millson asked.

Laura Stebbing's mouth suddenly went square-shaped. Her eyes squeezed shut and tears appeared under the lashes. Scrabbling at the clasp of her handbag, she opened it and pulled out a handkerchief. 'I—I'm sorry,' she whispered, dabbing her eyes. 'It's such a shock. We were . . . good friends . . . very close . . .' Her voice broke. She took a deep breath. 'I'll be all right in a minute,' she said.

'Take your time,' Millson said gently. 'There's no hurry.'

She nodded and took another breath. 'We've been working together for about three years . . . on the mobile library. We were so happy . . . so very happy.' The tears started again. 'She was such a nice person. Always . . .' She gulped, her voice faltering. 'Always cheerful. I just can't believe it. How was she killed?'

'We shall have to wait for the pathologist's report to know for sure, but it seems likely she was hit on the head.'

'Poor Janet.' Laura Stebbing's mouth quivered with emotion. 'Would she have suffered much?'

'I think she would have died very quickly,' Millson said reassuringly. 'She wouldn't have known much about it.'

'Oh, that's something then.' Laura Stebbing smiled weakly through her tears.

'When was the last time you saw her?'

'Yesterday evening when I dropped her off here at six o'clock after work.'

'The doctor believes she was killed some time last night. Can you give us any idea what she might have been doing in Tanniford? Who she might have been meeting?'

'No, no, I can't,' she said quickly.

'Are you sure?' Millson asked.

'Yes.'

'Did she have any men friends?'

Laura Stebbing hesitated as though uncertain how to answer. Then she said slowly, 'We meet a lot of people going round the villages. Janet was friendly with everyone, including the men. She didn't go out with any of them, though.'

'And you'd have known?' Millson pressed. 'Being close friends, I mean.'

She looked uncomfortable. 'Yes . . . at least, I think so.'

'Can you tell us about her family?' Scobie asked. 'They'll have to be informed.'

'She didn't have any family. She told me she was taken into care as a baby—back in the 'fifties—and didn't know who her parents were. You'd never know it, though. She wasn't bitter at all.'

'She never married?'

'No. She lived with a man for a while.'

'How long ago was this?'

'Oh, years ago. They had a joint mortgage. She told me when he left her she starved herself to keep up the payments and hang on to this house. She wasn't interested in trying with anyone else. Once bitten, twice shy, she said.'

Millson stood up. 'Thank you. We won't detain you any further, Mrs Stebbing. If you wouldn't mind giving the sergeant your address and telephone number. In the absence of relatives you may be asked to formally identify the body.'

Laura Stebbing gasped and her hand flew to her mouth. 'Oh dear, how awful. And I'll have to let them know in the office what's happened.' She wiped her eyes with the handkerchief. 'Oh, this is really terrible,' she said miserably.

Millson nodded sympathetically. Leaving Scobie to take a note of Laura Stebbing's details, Millson went upstairs. There was a bedroom and a bathroom above. The bedroom was fragrant with scent. A navy blue skirt and a white shirt-blouse similar to the clothes Mrs Stebbing was wearing had been left on the bed. A bra and a pair of briefs lay on the floor. Otherwise the room was neat and tidy.

He looked briefly in the wardrobe and the drawers of the dressing-table. There was nothing out of the ordinary, no sign of a male presence. Janet West clearly lived alone.

Downstairs, Scobie escorted Mrs Stebbing out of the front door and along the road to the coach. She opened the driver's door and clambered in.

'You drive this thing?' Scobie asked in surprise.

'Yes, of course. We both do . . . did.'

'Don't you need an HGV licence?'

'No, it weighs less than thirty-eight tons. You don't need one.' She started the engine.

'I forgot to ask,' Scobie said. 'Did Janet West own a car?'

She leaned out of the window. 'Yes, a red Fiat Panda. It's usually parked outside, but I don't see it here today.'

'Thanks.' Scobie made a note and returned to the house.

Millson was in the front room going through the drawers

of a small bureau desk. His hand came out holding an indexed address book.

'This is what I was looking for. And we'll take this too,' he said lifting a framed photograph from the top of the desk. It was of Janet West and Laura Stebbing standing in front of the library coach, arms round each other and smiling. 'We'll call in the office on the way back and have some copies run off.'

When Millson and Scobie returned to the shipyard, a police mobile incident room was being set up on the edge of the waste ground which was now half filled with cars. As they walked towards the police trailer a black BMW swept into the car park. A girl with short dark hair and wearing a grey gaberdine business suit jumped from the driving seat and strode forward to intercept them.

'Who are you two and what's going on here?' she demanded, stepping in front of Millson and forcing him to stop.

He looked down into dark blue eyes. 'I'm Detective Chief Inspector Millson and this is Detective-Sergeant Scobie. Who might you be?'

'Nicola Richmond. I own this shipyard.' She pointed at the Incident Room trailer. 'What's that thing doing here?'

A uniformed constable was placing a yellow sign, INCI-DENT ROOM against the side of the vehicle. 'You can see what it is, madam,' Millson said tartly, wondering how this slip of a girl came to own a shipyard.

'Yes, I can see perfectly well, Chief Inspector. What I want to know is why is it here?'

Millson resented being challenged by a peremptory young woman—shipyard owner or not—and he answered curtly. 'A woman's body has been found near here and I am about to begin a murder investigation. *That's* why it's here.'

Nicola Richmond's expression changed. 'A body? Here? In my yard?' Millson noted the possessive 'my'.

Scobie answered her. 'No. Along the riverbank towards Alresford.'

'Who is she?'

'Her name is Janet West,' Millson said. 'Do you know her?'

Nicola Richmond shook her head. 'When did it happen?'

'Late last night.'

'What was she doing on the riverbank late at night?'

'Presumably she was meeting someone,' Millson said tersely. 'A man.'

'Why do you say that?'

Angered by the continuous interrogation, Millson retorted, 'A woman doesn't doll herself up and wear exotic underwear to spend the evening alone.'

'How do you know what—?' Nicola Richmond stopped. 'Was she raped, then?' Her tone was unemotional.

Scobie saw Millson about to lose his temper completely and said quickly, 'That's for the pathologist to tell us and the information will be confidential until we release it to the public.'

The blue eyes switched to Scobie, appraising him. 'I see. Thank you.'

She turned on her heel and began walking away towards the shipyard entrance. After a few yards she stopped and turned round. 'If your officers would like to make use of the yard facilities my foreman will be glad to advise them, Chief Inspector,' she said in a conciliatory tone.

Millson unbent a little. 'Thank you, Mrs Richmond.'

'I'm not married,' she said, 'and if I were—' her mouth curved in a smile—'I wouldn't use my husband's name, I'd use my own.'

Millson nodded. That was no surprise to him. Nicola Richmond was a virago.

Scobie's thoughts about her were quite different. He was

intrigued by the shape of her mouth, small and bow-shaped, and was wondering what it would be like to kiss her.

As they continued towards the police trailer, Millson suddenly stopped. Head lifted, he began sniffing the air like a dog.

'Fried bacon,' Scobie said. 'It's coming from the shipyard canteen.'

'Did you have breakfast before you left this morning, Norris?'

'No.'

'Neither did I.' Millson and his daughter shared work in the kitchen. She prepared breakfast, he cooked dinner at night. This morning he'd missed out, though. His nostrils quivered. 'See if someone can rustle us up some bacon sandwiches and coffee. Miss Richmond said we were welcome to make use of the yard facilities.'

'I think she meant the loos,' Scobie said.

'Just do it, Norris! I'm famished.'

In the tiny office at the end of the Incident Room trailer, Millson and Scobie munched bacon sandwiches and examined the contents of two plastic bags brought to them by the exhibits officer. One contained Janet West's handbag and the other the items found on the ground around her body.

There was only her driving licence, a lipstick and some tissues in the handbag. As they tipped out the contents of the second plastic bag, Scobie separated some keys embossed with the Fiat logo from the cigarettes and other items.

'These must be her car keys. Mrs Stebbing told me Janet West owned a Fiat Panda. It wasn't outside her house.'

'She probably came here in her own car then, not someone else's,' said Millson. 'We need to find it.'

He stared thoughtfully at the items spread out on the table. 'No diary,' he commented. 'Most women carry a diary of some kind, if only to jot down the shopping list. Make a note to ask Mrs Stebbing if Janet West had one.'

As officers began telephoning the numbers in Janet West's address book, George Millson briefed his team of detectives in the middle section of the trailer which served as an operations room.

'We're awaiting the autopsy report,' he told them, 'but it's likely she was killed by a blow on the head. The police doctor reckons she'd been dead between five and ten hours—probably nearer ten—which puts the time of death roughly between nine o'clock and midnight. There was no indication of sexual assault. Robbery is a possibility. The contents of her handbag were scattered around the body and no money or credit cards were found. I'm keeping an open mind on that, though.'

He looked round the room. 'Who's assigned to press liaison?'

A WDC raised her hand. 'I'm police spokeswoman, sir.'

'Right. The only information we're releasing at the moment is that a woman's body has been found beside the river and we're treating her death as suspicious. We'll give further details after we've contacted her next of kin. It seems she may not have anyone, but we'd better make sure.'

He turned to a uniformed sergeant. 'I want a hands and knees search of the entire area where the body was found. You'll need to call in divers to search the riverbed. Specifically, we're looking for a diary and the murder weapon. It's likely to be something heavy like a brick or an iron bar.'

Millson continued, 'She drove a red Fiat Panda and it's most likely here in the village. We need to recover it and to find out what she was doing in Tanniford. Sergeant Scobie will be making the assignments and distributing copies of her photograph. We'll be visiting every house and pub in the village to ask if anyone saw her last night. A woman doesn't go walking along the river late at night on her own. She must have had someone with her. That someone was almost certainly a man.'

Millson added soberly, 'It's essential we find him.'

CHAPTER 4

A red Fiat Panda was located almost immediately, hemmed in by other vehicles parked on the waste ground. The keys found near Janet West's body fitted the locks and a check with PNC Hendon confirmed her ownership. Called from the Incident Room with Scobie, Millson poked his head inside the car. A pair of flat-heeled women's shoes lay on the floor on the driver's side. He withdrew his head.

'Looks as though she drove here on her own,' he commented. 'So the man she was meeting either lives in Tanniford or came here in his own car.' He addressed the constable who'd found the car. 'I doubt we'll gain any useful evidence from it, but have forensic check the vehicle over.' He turned to Scobie. 'Now, where did she go from here? Did she walk to someone's house? Or had they arranged to meet in a pub?'

'The Black Boy is the nearest,' Scobie said.

'Uh-huh.' Millson looked around him. In front of them was the shipyard and to their right the back gardens of houses. On their left, beyond the waste ground, a field bordering the shipyard ran down to the river.

'Well, whatever she did,' he said, 'we know where she ended up. And she certainly didn't tramp through that field of grass to get there. At some point in the evening she walked through the shipyard to the pedestrian gate on to the riverbank and then along the path to where she was killed. Is there another way into the yard besides the front entrance here?'

Scobie nodded. 'Yes, at the side. There's an eleven-foot-wide right of way all along the quay for the emergency services. But if she came from that direction she would still have to go through the yard to reach the riverbank.'

'Right. Then let's assume she entered from here.'

They threaded their way between the cars and walked through the shipyard entrance that was marked only by an iron pole mounted on a counterbalance between two sheds.

The yard, silent earlier that morning, was vibrant with activity. Overhead cranes were lifting heavy giant sheets of steel and manœuvring them into position on the decks of the vessel where welders were at work.

Millson and Scobie followed the right of way across the perimeter of the yard, indicated only by a cleared path through discarded sections of steel plate resembling huge jigsaw pieces. They went through the gate to the riverbank by the water's edge and continued along the path to where Janet West's body had been found. In the field, a line of men wearing plastic gloves were finger-searching the ground on hands and knees.

Millson gazed broodingly at the taped-off area of grass where the body had lain. The sun was shining brightly now, making the scene less sinister.

'What was she doing here, Norris? It was dark.'

'Maybe she met her date in a pub, they had a few drinks and then he brought her here for a spot of love-making,' Scobie suggested, recalling summer evenings beside the river with Kathy.

Millson's mouth twisted sceptically. 'At this time of year? Anyway, I doubt if a woman of her age, dressed in her best gear, is going to lie down in the grass for that. Unless, perhaps, he got her blind drunk first—and we shan't know that until the post-mortem.'

He shaded his eyes against the sun and peered downriver towards Alresford creek. 'What's that?' He pointed to a barge with a wooden hut on its deck, lying against the bank.

'It's a relic of the last war,' Scobie explained. 'The yard built concrete barges to carry fuel and water for the D-Day invasion. That's one that didn't get there. I believe the local scouts use it now.'

'Let's take a look at it.'

The barge had a rounded bow and stern. Over the years the flat-bottomed hull had churned a shallow berth in the mud of the riverbed so that it lay upright whatever the state of the tide. Rusty trapdoors in the flat deck gave access to the tanks below.

A large wooden hut had been erected on its deck at some time and was painted olive green. Barbed wire was strung through the stanchion posts along the edge of the deck, making a formidable barrier. Between two of the stanchions where a gangplank led from the deck to the bank, there was a gate secured with a padlock.

'Well, that disposes of one possibility,' Millson said. 'Janet West and her gentleman friend didn't nip up there to do their canoodling.'

'Unless it was the scoutmaster she was having it off with,' Scobie said with a grin. 'He'd have a key.'

There was no answering smile on Millson's face. 'Many a true word spoken in jest comes home to roost, Norris,' he said, in a shameless mishmash of sayings. 'Have a DC check where the scoutmaster was yesterday evening.'

News of the murder had spread among the yard's workforce and as the two policemen returned through the shipyard a small man in overalls, sideboards of grey hair showing below his protective helmet, approached them.

'Can I help you, gentlemen? I'm the foreman, Harry Tripp.'

'Yes. Tell me, can anyone walk through here at night?' Millson asked.

'Yep. There's a right of way along the river all the way from Colchester to Thorrington. One day Miss Richmond hopes to have it diverted outside our perimeter fence in return for building a proper footpath. That's what they done around the timber yard the other side of the village.'

'How did Miss Richmond come to own the shipyard?' Scobie asked curiously.

Harry Tripp's face broke in a grin. ''Cos her grandad—old man Richmond—worshipped her little toenails, that's how. He brought young Nicky up to take over when he died.'

Scobie was about to ask more about Nicola Richmond when Millson grunted impatiently and brought the foreman back to the matter of security. 'So the yard is completely open at night?'

'Yep, same as by day.'

'Is it lit at night?'

'Right of way is, not the rest.'

'Don't you get a lot of thieving?'

The foreman shook his head and grinned. 'Ain't much of a market for offcuts of steelplate, an' that's mostly what's lying around. The equipment is locked away in the sheds when the last shift finishes.' His face clouded. 'We've had some vandalism lately, though.'

'Isn't there a security guard?' Scobie asked.

'Sure there is, but he can't be everywhere.'

'Where's the man who was on duty last night?' Millson demanded. 'I'd like to speak to him.'

'He'll be sleeping now,' Harry Tripp said.

'No doubt,' said Millson, 'but where can we find him?'

'In Station Road—top of the High Street here. I don't know the number but his is the third house along. His name's Pearson, Leonard Pearson. He won't like being woke up from his sleep, though.'

'Nor did I first thing this morning,' Millson said sourly. As they walked up Tanniford's short High Street and neared the estate agent's at the corner with Station Road, Millson asked Scobie, 'Do you want to pop your head in and say hallo to your girlfriend, Norris?'

'No.' Scobie's tone was curt. 'We're having a cooling-off period at the moment.'

'Oh, why's that?'

'I asked her to make up her mind about marrying me.'

'So what's the problem?' Millson asked.

Scobie's expression became rueful. 'She said she wasn't going to be rushed and wanted to think things over. Kathy's not keen on marriage. She'd rather we just lived together. I wouldn't . . . I want us to be married.'

Millson shook his head wonderingly. 'In my day it was the girls who were keen to get married, not the men.'

Leonard Pearson's wife was a small, rotund woman with red cheeks and white hair.

'He's usually asleep at this time,' she said when Millson and Scobie introduced themselves on the doorstep. 'But that woman's murder's upset him something terrible and he doesn't feel like sleeping.'

'How did he hear about it?' Millson asked.

'The fisherman who found her used the phone in his office to call the police. Come in, he's in the kitchen.'

Pearson was in his mid-fifties, a heavily-built man with a few strands of brown hair brushed sideways over his otherwise bald head. Steel-framed spectacles surmounted a large nose. He waved Millson and Scobie to chairs and continued sipping a mug of tea.

'Did you know the dead woman?' Millson asked. 'Her name was Janet West?' Pearson shook his head and Millson went on, 'What time did you go on duty last night?'

'Seven o'clock. I does seven in the evening to seven in the morning. That's from when the late shift finishes till the early one comes on. I does alternate nights with the other guard, Tom Lowery. That way we gets different nights each week.'

'Uh-huh. And you patrol the yard during the night?'

'Yeh. I do a tour of the yard and the buildings every two hours. It's in me instructions. First one soon after seven to see everywhere's shut up. Then at nine, then eleven and so on.'

'And where are you in between times?'

'I has a small office wi' a gas ring in the shed 'longside the entrance barrier.'

Scobie looked up from making notes. 'Are you able to see the waste ground where they park the cars from there?'

'Yeh, most of it.'

'Did you see a red Fiat Panda there yesterday evening?'

'Can't say I did. All sorts of cars are parked there over-night on account of there's hardly anywhere to park in the village.'

Millson took up the questioning again. 'Did you notice anything out of the ordinary last night? Between nine o'clock and midnight, say?'

Pearson said positively, 'No. Nothing at all.'

'Did you see anyone using the right of way through the yard?'

'No, but then I wouldn't if I were on me rounds.'

'Do many people use that right of way?'

Pearson shrugged. 'Lads and lassies from the village sometimes. After the pubs close. Specially if it's a warm night.' His mouth twisted in a leer. 'Get up to all manner of tricks down there on the riverbank, they do.'

'But not last night?'

'Not that I knows of,' Pearson said.

At home that evening Millson relaxed in an armchair to consider the day's results.

At a table in the corner, Dena's dark head was bent over her homework, books spread out around her. There was a companionable silence between them and Millson was thankful that, unlike her mother, his daughter seemed to know instinctively when to leave him to his thoughts. A year ago he'd reorganized his life around her after she'd refused to live with his ex-wife and her husband any longer and moved in with him. He'd been prepared for problems in coping with a teenage daughter single-handed, but every-thing had gone smoothly so far.

The search of the riverbed and the adjoining fields had failed to discover the murder weapon or any further belongings of the dead woman; and the response to the house-to-house inquiries had been disappointing. A number of residents knew Janet West, though not always by name. Some of them knew her simply as 'the Book Lady' who visited houses in the village and exchanged books. No one had noticed her or her car in Tanniford yesterday evening.

The names and phone numbers in her address book had yielded nothing useful either. None of them were of relatives and most of the addresses were business addresses: hairdresser, dentist, plumber and so on.

Janet West's employers at library headquarters described their library assistant as a model employee to the WDC who called on them. She was efficient, never off sick and went to endless trouble to supply her readers with the books they asked for.

An unblemished character and not a sniff of a man in her life,' the WDC reported. 'Though I don't think they really knew much about what she did out of working hours.'

Janet West's neighbours had responded in similar terms. Janet was friendly and cheerful and they didn't think she had any menfriends. One of them, across the street from Janet's house, had seen her driving away in her car at eight-thirty yesterday evening.

'What about the scoutmaster?' Millson had asked Scobie before he left that evening.

'His name is Kevin Goodman. He says he was at home from nine o'clock onwards yesterday evening. The DC who called on him said he doesn't look the type to go out wenching.'

Millson pondered on why anyone would want to kill a respectable, well-liked woman like Janet West. He doubted she'd been killed in the course of robbery or rape. There was no jealous husband and she didn't have a lover, although he was sure she'd been meeting a man. Was that man her murderer? Or had she been killed before they met? Or after they parted?

Late afternoon there had been a phone message informing him that Laura Stebbing had formally identified Janet West's body and the warrant for the autopsy had been issued.

The police had to be represented at the post-mortem, but Millson had decided against attending himself. It was a long drive to the laboratory at Huntingdon and he didn't expect the report to be other than routine.

He was wrong about that. It contained a surprise.

CHAPTER 5

'There was post-mortem œdema on the shoulders and but-tocks,' the pathologist told Millson on the phone the next morning.

'What the heck does that mean?'

'It means the body was moved after death. She wasn't killed where you found her.'

Millson compressed his lips. This added a totally new perspective to the murder.

'She was killed by two heavy blows to the head, delivered by a round object like a metal bar,' the pathologist went on. 'The wounds were to the left frontal area of the head indicating they were delivered by a right-handed person standing in front of her. Not a frenzied attack. Deliberate blows intended to kill, I'd say.'

Death had occurred between nine o'clock and ten—prob-ably around nine-thirty—on Wednesday night. There were no indications of sexual assault or rape—no scratches on the thighs, no torn clothing and no blood or skin under her fingernails. However, there had been recent sexual inter-course.

'How recent?' Millson asked.

'Shortly before death. The spermatazoa were still quite lively. And she'd had a meal about two hours before. Do you want to know what it was?'

'No, thank you,' Millson said.

'This rules out a mugging,' he told Scobie as the team gathered for a fresh briefing later that morning. 'A mugger wouldn't stop to move his victim. He'd leave her and run like hell.'

'The body was moved,' Millson told his team. 'Which

means she was killed somewhere else and her body dumped there later. She weighed a hundred and twenty pounds, so she'd take some carrying and there were no signs she'd been dragged across the grass. Also, the laboratory found cement dust on the back of her raincoat and abrasions to the undersides of her thighs.' He looked round the gathering. 'It doesn't take a genius to work out that the body was taken there in a wheelbarrow used for building work.'

And that was the explanation for Janet West's clothes being in disarray, Millson realized. She'd been wheeled along the riverbank and tipped out like a load of rubbish. The thought angered him.

'Let's find it,' he went on. 'This morning we'll extend the search to the shipyard and the area around it. That's where the murder weapon is likely to be, too.'

After the briefing, Millson faced the waiting media assembled outside. He told reporters the murdered woman was Janet West, aged forty-two, a library assistant. She had been killed by blows to the head and although money was missing from her handbag, he was keeping an open mind as to the motive for her murder. There was reason to believe she was with a man Wednesday evening and it was vital the man came forward in order to be eliminated from the inquiries. Millson ended with an appeal for anyone with information to contact the Incident Room or their local police station. He made no mention of the body having been moved.

As he and Scobie re-entered the Incident Room a uniformed constable hurried up the steps behind them. 'The yard foreman's raising problems over the search, sir. He's refusing to let us start.'

'You deal with it,' Millson told Scobie. 'Tell him he'll be arrested for obstructing inquiries if he doesn't cooperate.' His eyes crinkled in an impish smile. 'Better still, get hold of Miss Bossy Boots and threaten *her* with arrest.'

In the yard Scobie found a uniformed sergeant engaged in heated argument with the yard foreman.

'What's the trouble?' Scobie asked.

'The foreman won't let us begin the search,' said the sergeant, 'he says it's too dangerous.'

The foreman pointed up at the arm of an overhead crane swinging sideways above their heads as it conveyed a metal sheet to the upper deck of the vessel. 'I can't have your men wandering around while them cranes are working.'

'Then stop them,' Scobie snapped.

The foreman's eyes bulged. '*Stop the cranes!* The yard would be brought to a standstill.'

'I can't help that,' Scobie said. 'The men have to search the area. This is a murder investigation and you're obstructing our inquiries. That's an offence.'

'Oh, is that so? Well, Miss Richmond will soon sort you lot out.' He raised an arm and signalled to a window in the office block at the entrance to the yard. 'Miss Nicola will have something to say about this. She sees everything goes on in the yard from up there.'

A moment later the slim figure of Nicola Richmond emerged from a door on the ground floor of the office block and came towards them.

'What's the problem, Harry?' she asked as she approached.

'These here police—'

Scobie broke in. 'We want to search the shipyard, Miss Richmond. We have reason to believe the murder weapon may be here. We'll be as quick as we can, but the search must be carried out. Your foreman refuses to stop the cranes so we can proceed.'

Nicola Richmond's eyebrows came together in a frown and she regarded Scobie steadily for a moment. He thought she was going to support the foreman until she nodded and said, 'Stop the cranes, Harry.'

'What? But—'

'Do as I say.' Her tone was that of a parent ordering a disobedient child to behave itself.

'Yes, Miss Richmond.' Harry Tripp walked away muttering.

'You must forgive Harry,' she said to Scobie. 'He's under a great deal of pressure. The launch is scheduled for the next spring tides in a fortnight's time. If we don't launch then we incur heavy penalty payments for late delivery.' The dark blue eyes met his. 'That would bankrupt me,' she said.

'You took your time,' Millson grumbled when Scobie rejoined him in his office.

'I thought it best to establish good relations with Miss Richmond,' Scobie said defensively. He'd spent pleasurable moments watching the movements of Nicola Richmond's kissable mouth as she told him of the financial problems she was up against.

'Is that what you were doing?' Millson's tone was caustic.

Scobie ignored the criticism. 'She's sacrificing precious time suspending operations for us. They're working to a very tight deadline. They have to launch at the top of the next spring tides.'

'*Spring* tides? Spring's come and gone, hasn't it?'

Scobie glanced at him, not sure if he was serious or making a joke. He decided to explain.

'Spring tides have nothing to do with the Spring. They occur every fortnight throughout the year. The tide rises higher and there's more water. Springs alternate with neap tides which rise and fall much less.'

'Is that a fact?' Millson said. He shook his head wonderingly. 'The things you know that I don't, Norris.'

Scobie stared at him suspiciously, still not sure whether Millson was mocking him.

The search of the shipyard ended at midday. Three wheelbarrows had been found, all of them in use. Workmen were trundling them back and forth between a cement mixer and a crumbling area of concrete that was being renewed. The barrows had been left upturned beside the mixer at the end of the day on Wednesday. They had been in use again yesterday and today and there was no point in examining them for forensic evidence now.

Some pieces of iron bar and pipework lying about had been collected together and sent for forensic examination. None of them looked likely to be the murder weapon, though.

'Why d'you think he moved her body, Norris?' Millson asked over a lunch of beer and sandwiches at the Spread-eagle. The Spreadeagle was along Anglesea Road from the shipyard, on the corner of a lane to a pedestrian crossing over the railway tracks.

'I suppose it's too obvious to say because he didn't want her found where he'd killed her?'

'No. No, that's exactly the point. *Where* he killed her is significant. I believe it was in the shipyard. And that's why she was moved . . . to divert suspicion from there. Which is also the reason the killer tried to make things look as though she'd been mugged.'

When they returned from lunch, a visitor was waiting to see Millson.

'He insists on speaking to you personally, sir. I couldn't get out of him what it was about,' a WPC explained apologetically. 'He's an old fart . . . eighty if he's a day.'

Millson eyed her sternly. She was very young. 'At what age do people become old farts, Constable?'

'Sir?' She stared at him. 'I . . . er . . .' Her cheeks flushed.

'I take it this elderly gentleman is in possession of all his faculties, Constable.'

'Er—yes, sir. Yes, I would say so.'

'In that case, wheel him in.' Millson's face relaxed in a smile. 'And try to remember you'll be old yourself one day. So, a little more tolerance towards senior citizens. Eh, Constable?'

'Yessir.' She about-turned smartly and marched out.

Harold Smith was seventy-nine—or so he said. He had thin white hair and moved awkwardly as he entered Millson's office. 'Arthritis,' he grumbled, using his stick to lower himself on to a chair.

Millson gave him an encouraging smile. 'I'm the officer in charge of the case, Mr Smith. What did you want to speak to me about?'

'The . . . Book . . . Lady.' Harry Smith spoke so slowly that Scobie wondered if he suffered from a mental handicap.

'What about her?' Millson asked.

A pause of several seconds and then, 'She were with me Wednesday.'

Millson was reminded of the time he'd interviewed a patient in a psychiatric hospital. The man had moved and spoken like a film in slow motion and a nurse had explained that he was undergoing narco-analysis—psychoanalysis with drugs.

'What time Wednesday?' Scobie asked.

'Four to quarter-past. She brought me a book from the library.'

They waited. Then, as that seemed to be the extent of Harry Smith's information, Millson said, 'Well, thank you for coming, Mr—'

'That weren't all,' Harry Smith said, with maddening slowness.

They waited again.

'She were going out that evening.' Harry Smith's jaws began a chewing motion, as though he had food in his mouth.

'Yes?' Millson prompted when the movements ended.

'In Tanniford.'

'We know that.' Millson took a breath to control his impatience and said coaxingly, 'Tell us exactly what she said, Harry.'

The warm tone and the use of his first name seemed to lubricate Harry Smith's thought processes. His face opened in a grin and his words flowed more readily. 'I asked her if she had a date that night, 'cos if not I wanted to take her out.'

Millson looked down and concentrated on his toecaps. If Harry, aged seventy-nine—and Millson suspected he was even older than that—had the temerity to ask out a smart woman of forty-two, it was not to be smiled at, especially after the lecture he'd given the young constable.

'Y'see, I'd seen her here in her car before on a Wednesday night.'

Millson's eyes leapt up from his toecaps like a Harrier jump-jet. 'When?'

Harry Smith's wrinkled forehead creased in thought, adding further wrinkles. After a while he said, 'Reckon it were two weeks ago and again two weeks afore that.'

'And you're sure it was always a Wednesday?' Millson pressed.

'Oh yeh, 'cos I had the dog with me.'

Millson waited for enlightenment. When it didn't come he asked, 'Why does that make it a Wednesday, Harry?'

'I goes to the Black Dog on Wednesday nights an' they won't have dogs in the bar no more. He don't like being on his own an' I take him to me sister's.'

'Where did you see Janet on those two Wednesdays?'

'Driving down the High Street.'

'What time would this be?'

'Nine o'clock. That's the time I takes the dog for a piddle in the churchyard on the way to me sister's.'

'What about this last Wednesday?'

'I didn't see her then. I was late getting out.'

Disappointed, Millson sat back in his chair and gave a nod to Scobie.

'So what did Janet say when you asked if she had a date?' Scobie asked.

'She jes' looked at me an' said, "We all have our secrets, Harry."' He let out a brief cackle. 'She were right about that. I kep' on asking her to come out with me, but she wouldn't.'

'What else did you and Janet talk about?'

'Nothing.'

Scobie scanned his notes. According to Harry, Janet West had been with him for a quarter of an hour. 'Surely there was more conversation than that, Mr Smith?'

'Nope.'

'What were you doing for the rest of the time, then?' Scobie's voice was jocular.

'Listening. She were reading to me.' His eyes slid from Scobie to Millson. 'Jes' reading,' he repeated.

'*What* was she reading?' Millson asked.

'Oh . . . I dunno.' Harry Smith shrugged. His eyes were evasive.

'Oh, come on, Harry,' Millson insisted, intrigued now.

'I don't remember,' Harry said stubbornly.

It could be of no consequence, Millson thought. Suddenly, Harry became eloquent.

'She was magic, was the Book Lady . . . sheer magic. She had this lovely voice, see . . . like Marlene Dietrich. It carried you away . . .' He was hunched forward, eyes closed and his hands between his thighs, squeezing his knees together. 'Wonderful, she was. Warm . . . kind . . .'

His eyes opened and he stopped. Abruptly, he said, 'She were a very nice lady an' I hopes you gets the bastard who done her in. Thass all I gotta say.'

He grabbed his stick, pushed himself to his feet and walked out stiffly. Millson stared after him thoughtfully.

'The way Harry tells it,' said Scobie, 'it sounds as though

Janet West had a regular date with a man who lives in Tanniford. None of the pubs or eating places recognized her picture, so presumably she didn't meet him for a drink or a meal.'

'And Laura Stebbing said she didn't have any men friends.' Millson stroked his cheek. 'The two of them working together—close friends—*very* close friends, according to Laura Stebbing—and Janet didn't let fall a hint—not one single word—about this man? I don't believe it!' Millson snapped. 'I want to speak to Mrs Stebbing. Where can we get hold of her?'

Scobie rummaged in his briefcase and brought out a yellow leaflet. 'I picked up a timetable from the library.' He unfolded it. 'Mobile 3 . . . Friday . . . here we are.' He glanced at his watch. 'She's due at Great Bentley at three-forty-five.'

CHAPTER 6

At Great Bentley, Millson turned his car off the road and drove across its immense village green to the yellow library coach standing on the far side.

Laura Stebbing looked up from the counter as Millson and then Scobie filled the centre doorway.

'Goodness, this is a surprise, Chief Inspector. What are you doing here?'

'I'd like to ask you some questions, Mrs Stebbing.' Millson's eyes swept the coach. It was empty except for a man sitting in the driver's seat behind Laura Stebbing. 'Perhaps we could talk in my car.'

'Yes. All right.' She turned and spoke to the man behind her. 'Take over for a while, Bill.' She lifted a flap in the counter and squeezed through it. 'Bill Bragg is Janet's replacement,' she explained as she stepped down from the coach. 'He worked with Janet when I was on holiday last year.'

Millson nodded and spoke quietly over his shoulder to Scobie. 'See what Mr Bragg can tell you about Janet West. And ask him about her voice.'

'Her voice?' Scobie looked perplexed.

'Ask him if she had a sexy voice,' Millson muttered impatiently. He turned away and escorted Laura Stebbing to his car. 'You're not very busy today,' he commented, opening the door for her.

'No, it's like this sometimes. Even when we're busy it doesn't really need two people to operate the library,' she said.

Millson edged himself in beside her in the rear seat and took out his cigarettes.

'I don't smoke,' she said when he offered them to her. 'I

don't mind a bit if you do, though,' she added quickly as he went to put them away. 'Janet used to smoke,' she said wistfully. Her head drooped. 'I do so miss her.'

'I'm sure you do,' Millson said sympathetically. He finished lighting a cigarette. 'You told me Janet didn't have a manfriend, Mrs Stebbing.'

'That's right, she didn't.'

'Well, we now have a witness who saw Janet in Tanniford in her car on two previous Wednesday evenings. Which suggests she was meeting someone regularly. Did she give you any hint of who she was going out with?'

Laura Stebbing's mouth set obstinately. 'She wasn't going out with anyone. Why should it be a *man* she was meeting?'

'Because she had sex with him,' Millson said bluntly.

Laura Stebbing's eyes widened. 'I don't believe it! Who says so?'

'The pathologist says so in the autopsy report.'

'Oh.' She looked down and began plucking nervously at her skirt. 'I can't understand it,' she muttered.

'D'you know a man called Harry Smith?' Millson asked.

She looked up. 'Yes, he belongs to the library.'

'Mr Smith told us Janet came to his house and read to him last Wednesday afternoon when the library was in Tanniford. Can you confirm that?'

She nodded. 'Janet used to read to lots of the older borrowers. And she changed their books for them to save them walking to the coach.' She turned her head to him. 'I know it sounds corny, Chief Inspector, but Janet had a genuine love of old people.'

'It doesn't sound corny to me, Mrs Stebbing,' Millson assured her. 'I gather they were very fond of her too. Certainly Mr Smith was. Though he was shy of telling us what Janet was reading to him. Do you know what it was?'

'*The Thousand and One Nights*.' With a faint smile she added, 'An unexpurgated version.'

Millson's eyebrows rose. 'I'm surprised you carry a book like that on your shelves.'

'We don't. Janet put in a special request for it. We don't lend it out.'

She looked away from him and out of the window. 'Some of our older readers are very lonely, Mr Millson. Their wives may have died . . . or they're divorced . . . separated perhaps. Janet brought a sparkle into their lives . . . and they appreciated that.'

Millson waited for her to say more. When she remained silent he said, 'So you minded the library and Janet did Samaritan work?'

Without turning her head she murmured, 'As I said, it doesn't take two to operate the library.'

Millson drew on his cigarette, reflecting on her words. After a moment he said, 'Mr Smith told us he asked Janet if she had a date that night and she replied: "We all have our secrets." What d'you think she meant by that?'

Laura Stebbing's head turned back from the window. 'I don't suppose she meant anything. It was probably her way of putting him off when he asked to take her out."

'What did she usually do with her evenings? Did she go out to pubs?'

'Good heavens no!' Laura Stebbing was shocked. 'Janet wouldn't dream of such a thing. Sometimes we'd go to the cinema or theatre together . . . or have a meal out. She never went out on her own.'

'Well, she met this man somehow,' Millson insisted. 'Could it have been through the library? One of the men she read to, perhaps? She refused Harry Smith, but might she have accepted one of the others?'

'I doubt it. And anyway, she would have told me.'

'Do you know if Janet carried a diary in her handbag?'

'Yes, she did. She wrote down her appointments in it. She was very well organized.' Laura Stebbing's hands were twisting nervously in her lap. 'This man Janet met . . . he might have nothing to do with her death, might he?'

'That's possible. But if so, he should have come forward.'

'Perhaps he's married.'

'We've promised complete confidentiality,' Millson said.

'Well, perhaps he's too embarrassed . . . or ashamed.'

Millson frowned. 'About what?'

'About what his wife would say,' Laura Stebbing said quickly. Millson believed she had been thinking of something else, though.

'These men Janet used to read to, Mrs Stebbing. Would you have their names?'

She seemed taken aback. 'Er—some of them perhaps. Not all.'

'Well, do you keep records of who belongs to the library?'

'Ye-es.' Her expression was apprehensive. 'They're on the coach.'

'I'd like to see them,' Millson said, opening the car door.

'Very well.' Reluctantly, she stepped out.

In the coach she indicated a card index at the side of the counter. 'All the names and addresses are filed in there.'

'Fine. We'll borrow it.' He signalled to Scobie who was speaking to Bragg.

Laura Stebbing looked alarmed. 'Oh, I don't think I can allow—'

'It's Friday,' Millson said briskly. 'I'll have it returned to you first thing Monday morning. I don't imagine you'll need the cards over the weekend. If you're worried about releasing them, Sergeant Scobie can call up your office on the carphone.'

'No, no, that won't be necessary,' she said hurriedly. 'Take them.'

'What did Bragg have to say?' Millson asked Scobie as they drove away.

'Not a lot. He said Janet was friendly and very popular especially with the older borrowers. "Her little boys," she

called them. I asked him about her voice. He described it
as soft . . . husky. Said he supposed it could be a turn-on
for some men. What d'you want me to do with the card
index?'

'Go through it and take out the cards of the male borrowers. Janet West may have met this man through the
library. So we'll put the team to work over the weekend
questioning every man in that index. One other thing. Ask
the press liaison girl to put out an appeal for Janet West's
diary. Mrs Stebbing said Janet had one in her bag and
wrote her appointments in it. It's possible the killer took it
because his name was in it.'

On Saturday morning Scobie handed out index cards like
a teacher giving out homework. There had been over five
hundred men in the index, spread over twenty-seven
villages.

'Mistley—who's doing Mistley?' A DC raised his hand.
'Another one for you.' Scobie flicked a card to him.

Scobie finished distributing the cards and Millson stood
up and spoke to the team.

'Many of these men are pensioners and senior citizens,
so don't go charging around upsetting them. The dead
woman was well liked and they'll be keen to help. Make a
note of anyone who isn't. It's possible one of these men was
Janet West's date on Wednesday, so ask where they were
between nine and ten that evening and if they ever went
out with her. And see if they have any ideas on what she was
doing in Tanniford or who she might have been meeting.'

He went on, 'A witness has reported seeing her in Tanniford twice before on a Wednesday evening. So maybe Wednesday is significant. Anyone any thoughts on that?'

A WDC raised her hand. 'It could be the man's night
off, sir . . . the man she was meeting. He could be a barman
or something like that.'

'That's possible.' Millson pointed to a DC. 'Stenson,

you're local. What goes on here on Wednesdays the rest of us don't know about?'

'Well, I believe the scouts meet on Wednesdays, sir.' There was a ripple of laughter.

'Where?' Millson asked.

'In the scouts' hut . . . the one on the barge, sir. I think they meet once a fortnight from eight till nine.'

'Was there a meeting last Wednesday?'

'I don't know, sir.'

Millson looked round the room. 'Who interviewed the scoutmaster on Thursday?'

Another DC spoke up. 'I did, sir. He didn't say anything about a meeting, only that he was at home from nine o'clock onward on Wednesday.'

'Where does he live?'

'Just up Anglesea Road here.'

'Right. See if he's home this morning. If he is and he says there was a meeting Wednesday evening, tell him I'd like to see over the barge right away.'

Kevin Goodman was short and tubby and had spectacles. He wore a fawn pullover and khaki trousers and his black hair was brushed straight back from the forehead. His cheeks were smooth and pink and he had bright blue eyes. He could have been any age between thirty and fifty.

'I don't see how the scouts' hut can have anything to do with that poor woman's murder, Chief Inspector,' he said as he met Millson and Scobie on the riverbank.

'That's what we're here to look into,' Millson said crisply. 'Her body was found about a hundred yards away and the scouts were meeting here shortly before she was killed.'

Kevin Goodman's cheeks turned a deeper shade of pink. 'Oh, I see.' He mounted the gangplank and fitted a key to the padlock on the gate at the top. 'It's to keep out vandals,' he explained as he unlocked it. 'Though someone who was determined to get in could buy a key at any ironmonger's.'

Millson and Scobie followed him along the flush deck of the barge to the hut in the middle. Goodman unlocked the door and they stepped inside. There was one large room with tables and chairs and an old flower-patterned sofa. At one end there were doors to a toilet and kitchen.

Unexpectedly, Goodman sat down on the sofa. 'The vicar's wife donated this,' he said.

Millson and Scobie took a fold-up chair each.

'How many boys were here on Wednesday, Mr Goodman?' Millson asked.

'Er . . . twelve, I think. Yes, twelve. I remember thinking they made a nice round dozen.' His cheeks filled out in a smile.

'And what time did the meeting end?'

'Nine o'clock sharp.'

'Why did you tell the officer who called on you that you were at home at nine o'clock?'

'Because I was. Well . . . more or less. Certainly only a few minutes after.' Goodman glanced anxiously at Scobie writing in his notebook.

'*Minutes* after?' Millson asked. 'You live in Anglesea Road, don't you?'

'Yes, but I took a short cut home across the field.'

Millson stood up. 'Show me.'

Goodman went to a window and pointed to a row of houses on the other side of the field. 'My house is the one with the conservatory,' he said.

Millson stood with him, gazing across the field. 'Do you always go home that way?'

The scoutmaster hesitated. 'No, not in the dark. But there was a TV programme I was particularly keen to see.'

'Can anyone confirm the time you arrived home?'

Goodman looked worried. 'No. My wife wasn't home. Wednesday is her WI evening.'

'Uh-huh.' Millson returned to his chair. 'Did you know

Janet West?' he asked as Goodman resumed his seat on the couch.

'Only to speak to.' He gabbled an explanation. 'I manage a sports shop in Colchester and Wednesday is our half day, so I sometimes call in the library when it comes here in the afternoon.'

'Did you do so last Wednesday?'

'No, no, I didn't.' Goodman had begun to perspire.

'Did Janet West ever come to your home and read to you?'

Kevin Goodman looked startled. 'No, of course not. Why should she?'

'Just a thought,' Millson said. 'I'd like the names and addresses of the boys who were at your meeting.'

'What for, for goodness' sake?'

Millson said evenly, 'Scouts are supposed to be keen and alert at all times, aren't they? Isn't that what you teach them? These boys were on their way home from here not long before the murder was committed, so it's reasonable to assume one of them may have seen something.'

'Yes, I understand. I'm sorry, I didn't think.' Goodman went to a drawer in one of the tables and returned with an exercise book.

Scobie took it from him and copied out the names and addresses. When he finished, Millson stood up. 'Mind if we take a look around, Mr Goodman?'

'No, that's all right.' But as Millson and Scobie began looking in the cupboards, Goodman jumped up. 'I didn't realize you meant to carry out a search,' he said.

'Do you object?' Millson asked.

'No . . . no, it's OK. I was surprised, that's all.'

There was a suitcase in the bottom of one of the cupboards. 'Yours?' Scobie asked Goodman.

'Yes . . . it's a spare uniform,' the scoutmaster said quickly.

He followed them outside as they walked round the deck.

At the rear of the hut a wheelbarrow lay on its side.

'What's this for, Mr Goodman?' Millson asked.

'We use it to carry our rubbish to the village tip. I won't allow the boys to throw anything in the river.'

'What d'you make of him, Norris?' Millson asked as they returned along the riverbank.

'I can't see him as a killer. He seems quite harmless.'

'So do lots of men who murder women,' Millson reminded him. 'We've only his word he went home immediately after the scouts' meeting. He could be the man Janet met on Wednesday. Let's suppose he stays behind when the meeting's over and she comes here after the boys have left. He had time to kill her, wheel her body away and cut across the field home before his wife returned from her WI meeting.'

'With respect, that's all hypothesis and no evidence,' Scobie said.

'I agree. No motive either,' Millson added gloomily.

There was a message from Nicola Richmond at the Incident Room requesting Chief Inspector Millson to be kind enough to call at her office.

'You go, Norris. I have to run Dena to the station. She's spending the weekend with her mum,' Millson told Scobie.

George Millson's relationship with his ex-wife had improved a little since the bitter days of their custody battle. He now encouraged Dena to visit her occasionally, believing it was wrong for a daughter to lose contact with her mother entirely.

On the barge, Kevin Goodman lifted out the suitcase Scobie had noticed and laid it on the sofa. Unlocking it, he took out a neatly-folded girl guide's uniform. It was complete with skirt, blouse, scarf, beret, and navy blue pants. He went into the kitchen and peeled a large refuse bag from a roll lying on the floor. Returning to the sofa, he stuffed the guide's outfit into the bag and knotted the neck. Taking a clasp knife from his pocket, he stabbed holes in the bag and carried it out on deck. He looked around to make sure he was unobserved, then hurled the bag far out into the river.

It floated away on the outgoing tide, slowly filling with water until eventually it sank below the surface.

CHAPTER 7

Nicola Richmond stood up from the Victorian partners' desk that had been her grandfather's and went to the window of her office overlooking the shipyard. Last night, in a deliberate act of sabotage, someone had sawn through the cable of one of the jib cranes bringing much of the welding to a standstill. The launch date of the vessel whose bow towered above her window was now further at risk.

She turned and studied the critical path network on the wall. Two days ago, painting had become the critical activity and she had taken some welders off welding and put them on to painting. The problem was that the critical path had now moved to welding and although welders had made reasonable painters, painters were not capable of doing welding.

Nicola returned to her desk and looked up at the portrait of her grandfather on the wall above.

'Someone is trying to ruin me, Bertie,' she told the picture.

Nicola had begun calling her grandfather by his first name when she was twelve. It was a familiarity he himself had insisted upon when she and her father went to live with him after her mother died.

Bertram Richmond, whose wife had died some years earlier, had been delighted to have his son and granddaughter join him in the rambling house at Frating. From the beginning he took a keen interest in Nicola's upbringing and she soon discovered all the major decisions in her life were being made by Bertram Richmond and not her easygoing father, Philip.

Her years at Frating were happy and regulated. Each day, the chauffeur drove her father to the station at Alresford where he caught the train to Liverpool Street and his accountant's job in the City. The chauffeur then drove her grandfather to the shipyard at Tanniford and took Nicola on to her school in Colchester.

In the school holidays she often accompanied her grandfather to the yard where she would gaze up in awe at the great ribbed skeleton of a ship under construction. These leviathans fascinated the young Nicola and in time she became infused with her grandfather's love of building them.

Growing up in a male-only household had inevitable consequences. Not only was Nicola spoiled but, being a strong-minded girl, she made herself mistress of the house and its staff.

It was her grandfather's decision that she should study business administration at nearby Essex University instead of a university further afield, because he wanted to keep her at home with him. When she graduated three years later, he made her his office manager at the shipyard.

Two years on, as Bertram Richmond poured himself a glass of his favourite port, he was racked by a sudden pain in his chest. He died of a massive coronary before the ambulance reached hospital.

There was a knock at the door. Nicola Richmond's dark eyebrows lifted as her secretary showed in Scobie and she saw that he was alone. She looked beyond him with a wry smile.

'Is your master not with you?'

'The Chief Inspector is not available at the moment,' Scobie said uncomfortably. 'What did you want to see him about?'

She beckoned him to the window. Looking down, he saw below them in the yard the vivid blue flashes of arc-welding and the less obvious flares of gas-welding. A crane was lifting a heavy piece of equipment into place on the bridge-deck of the vessel.

Nicola Richmond rested her arms on the window-ledge, her face pressed against the glass. 'There's less than a fortnight to the launch now and someone is bent on preventing it.'

'How d'you mean?' Scobie asked.

'Look down there!' She pointed to a crane that was motionless. On the ground beneath it men were laying out wire cable. 'Last night someone sawed half through the cable with a hacksaw. This morning the cable broke lifting a capstan winch into the bow. It was a miracle no one was hurt.'

Scobie frowned. 'Your foreman mentioned you'd had trouble with vandals. I didn't realize it was this serious.'

'This wasn't vandalism, it was sabotage!' she said fiercely. 'Deliberate sabotage to cause delay and prevent us completing on time.'

'Are you sure?'

'Oh, I'm sure,' she said grimly. 'This is not the first incident. The others seemed like accidents. I know now they weren't.'

'Who would have an interest in delaying the launch?'

She turned and put her hands behind her on the sill. It had the effect of thrusting her body forward, outlining small firm breasts under the silk blouse.

'A developer called Andrew Hartman. He's trying to acquire this land so he can close the yard and build a housing estate on it. He approached me twelve months ago and I told him I wouldn't sell, whatever the price. He knows that if I default on the launch date I'll have to pay swingeing penalties under the contract and I'll be finished . . . broke. And that would suit Mr Hartman fine because I'd be forced to sell then.'

She saw Scobie take out his notebook and begin writing. 'I've no proof it's him,' she said.

Scobie nodded and went on writing. 'Is there anyone else who'd like to see you forced out of business?'

'Oh yes.' Nicola smiled crookedly. 'My stepmother. She'd love it.'

Five years ago, at the age of forty-five, Nicola's father had remarried. His new wife, Melissa, had been twenty-five, only two years older than his daughter. Nicola's grandfather was outraged. Nicola herself thought her father was foolish, not because Melissa was twenty years his junior, but because she didn't believe the girl loved him.

The newly-weds set up home in Findlesham, across the river from Tanniford. Nicola visited them a few times, but Melissa showed no desire to become friends with her stepdaughter and after a while Nicola stopped going.

She became absorbed in the work of the shipyard and was given ever wider responsibilities by her grandfather. 'One day you'll be managing all this, Nicky,' he told her.

She had assumed he meant under his direction, perhaps as yard manager, and she was stunned by his will read out by Lloyd Roberts, the family solicitor, in the oak-beamed sitting-room at Frating after the funeral.

In bewilderment she heard the words: *I bequeath my entire estate to my beloved granddaughter, Nicola* ... before Lloyd Roberts's voice was drowned by a scream of 'NO!' from Melissa Richmond. 'He can't have! The bastard can't have done that to us.'

Sitting next to her, Philip Richmond was glassy-eyed with shock. He'd known his father disapproved of him and his marriage to Melissa, but he'd never dreamed he would cut him out of his will completely.

'It's not right! We'll fight it!' Melissa was shouting and shaking his arm. 'You must fight it, Philip! She can't take *everything*.'

The solicitor's dry voice cut across her ranting. 'I can see no grounds upon which you could contest the will, Mrs Richmond.'

'Oh, can't you? Well, I can.' Melissa pointed a shaking

finger at Nicola. 'She seduced him! He was besotted with her.'

Not yet recovered from shock herself, Melissa's outburst struck Nicola like a douche of cold water. She had never analysed the close relationship with her grandfather, a relationship that had become closer still after her father left. Bertram Richmond had often told her she reminded him of her mother with whom, Nicola suspected, he'd been secretly in love. Perhaps she'd been naïve and Bertie's feelings for her had run deeper than she'd realized. So what? Nicola braced her shoulders. She wasn't going to cast her mind back over every caress and every intimacy to test the truth of Melissa's twisted accusations. To do so would be to sully the memory of that love between her and her grandfather.

'He was bewitched . . . completely under her influence,' Melissa was saying. 'The old fool didn't know what he was doing when he made that will.'

Lloyd Roberts's tone was acid. 'He most assuredly did, Mrs Richmond, as I myself would testify.'

Nicola's eyes were on her father, trying desperately to signal that she had been unaware of the will's contents and was as dumbfounded as he was. She was fond of her father, although she resented his weakness in not standing up to her grandfather and in taking so little interest in her.

He gazed back at her with the eyes of a wounded animal. Beside him, Melissa's face was white with fury.

'My stepmother hates me,' Nicola told Scobie. 'She thinks I did my father out of his inheritance because Grandfather left everything to me and nothing to him. She'd been expecting a bonanza when he died. I wouldn't be surprised if that was the only reason Melissa married my father.' Her eyes met his. 'She's my age, you see.' She moved away from the window and towards her desk. 'Anyway, I'd like a police guard on this place at night to prevent any further attacks until the ship is launched. That's what I was going to ask the Chief Inspector.'

'That's a matter for the local police,' Scobie said. 'We're here on a murder investigation.'

'You don't think there could be a link?'

'Between the sabotage and the killing of Janet West?' Scobie asked in surprise.

'Yes. Whoever is doing the damage could have been here Wednesday night. Perhaps she disturbed him as she walked through the yard and he killed her to prevent her identifying him. That's possible, isn't it?'

'What makes you think she was killed in the yard?' Scobie asked cautiously.

'Oh come, Sergeant, it's obvious you think that too from the way your men were swarming over it yesterday morning examining the wheelbarrows.'

'That doesn't mean her killer was your intruder. I agree it's possible, but I don't think it's very likely. In any case, it doesn't justify putting a police guard on the yard.'

Her mouth shaped in a pout. 'You're not being very helpful, Sergeant.'

Scobie relented. 'I tell you what, I'll put it to the Chief Inspector and see what he says, Miss Richmond.'

She smiled. 'Thank you. And please stop calling me Miss Richmond. I'm Nicola.' The blue eyes lifted to his. 'And you're Norris, aren't you? That's what I heard Mr Millson call you.' She held out her hand.

Scobie took the hand, experiencing a sudden urge to keep hold and shatter her composure by pulling her into his arms and crushing that kissable mouth with his own to see what she would do.

The phone call that afternoon was no surprise to Nicola Richmond.

'Mr Hartman is on the line, Miss Richmond,' her secretary informed her.

Andrew Hartman had made his first contact a year ago. He'd invited her to lunch and she'd accepted, believing it was best to deal with an enemy face to face. She'd expected an oily, smooth-talking man in a business suit and was disconcerted to meet a giant with a lazy smile who wore a flamboyant open-necked shirt. Andrew Hartman was about forty, with bushy, iron-grey hair. The friendly, easy-going manner belied his power and influence. In the exclusive restaurant where they dined, Nicola noticed he'd only to raise an eyebrow and a waiter came hurrying to attend him.

She listened politely as he outlined his scheme to develop the shipyard site with modern and attractive riverside properties.

'Holiday homes for Londoners, you mean,' said Nicola, 'Not homes for local people. If the shipyard closes the shops will close and the village will die. It's happening all over East Anglia. I won't let it happen in Tanniford. The men who work there and their families depend on me.'

'Shipbuilding is a dying business,' he retorted. 'You can't keep the yard going for ever.'

'It's been through hard times before. There's been ship-building of one kind or another at Tanniford for four hundred years. I'm not going to be the one to end it. I'm not selling,' she said firmly.

'Just tell me how much you want,' he persisted.

'I won't sell at any price. Don't you understand?'

'No, I don't,' he said. 'You'd be a very rich woman.'

She said frostily, 'Unlike you, Mr Hartman, money is not the most important thing in the world to me.'

Unperturbed by her criticism, he said, 'You'll have to sell some time. The yard's in bad shape with the recession in shipbuilding.'

'I'll survive,' Nicola said.

'Look,' he said impatiently, 'I came to you first because

you're chairman of the company and the largest share-holder. If you won't see sense I'll speak to the other share-holders.'

'It won't do you any good,' she'd told him. 'I hold the majority vote.'

That hadn't been strictly true. Her grandfather had left her his controlling interest of fifty-five per cent of the shares in the private company. The other forty-five per cent were in three blocks of fifteen per cent held by the widow and descendants of the three men who'd financed his purchase of the shipyard fifty years ago. Three months after Bertram Richmond's death, in a rush of guilt at her father's humiliation over the will, Nicola transferred to him a fifteen per cent block from her own holding. It put him on equal footing with the other three shareholders and left her with only forty per cent. The gesture was symbolic more than financial since the shares were currently not worth a great deal.

She made it clear to her father the transfer was to make no difference to her control of the business and she expected him always to vote with her at shareholders' meetings.

He'd been embarrassingly grateful. 'Oh, of course, Nicky, of course,' he said earnestly. 'You can count on me. I wouldn't let you down.'

Andrew Hartman had telephoned her twice since their lunch together and each time she had given him the same answer. The yard was not for sale at any price.

Then, last Wednesday, she had received a formal request from the other three shareholders for an extraordinary meeting to be held on Wednesday week after the launch of the *Vivacity*.

She lifted the receiver. 'The answer is still no, Mr Hartman,' she said, before he even spoke.

'I've made some inquiries. You'll go under if you don't land another order. The final payment for the present ship will barely keep you going—assuming you finish on time. If you don't, it's curtains for you.'

'We'll finish on time,' she said through her teeth. 'Despite your attempts to prevent us.'

'What are you talking about?'

'A fortnight ago it was a fire in the paint shop. Last night it was damage to a crane.'

'Are you accusing me of being responsible for these incidents?' he asked icily.

'No, I don't have the proof. But you're the only person who would benefit if I default on this order.'

He said angrily, 'Now you listen to me and listen good, young woman! I've spoken to the other shareholders and they're keen to sell. They'll put my proposition forward at the meeting they've called.'

'The decision will still be no,' Nicola snapped. 'I have a majority holding.'

'Oh no you don't,' he retorted. 'You only have forty per cent. Your father has the other fifteen per cent.'

Nicola frowned. How had he found that out?

'It comes to the same thing. My father always votes with me.'

'His wife thinks he might not this time.'

A chill came over Nicola. She kept her voice steady. 'You've spoken to my stepmother?'

'Of course. I've spoken to anyone who might further my cause.'

'My father will vote with me,' Nicola said, her voice shaking, 'whatever my stepmother thinks.'

'Well, my offer still stands—and it's very generous in the circumstances. You'll find I won't be so generous again and you'll end up having to sell to me at a knock-down price.'

'Stuff you!' Nicola said coarsely.

'Temper, temper.' He laughed and hung up.

*

Nicola Richmond picked up the phone. She rarely phoned her father, but this was an emergency. His presence and support at the shareholders' meeting was vital.

Melissa answered. 'This is Nicola Richmond,' Nicola said. 'I'd like to speak to my father, please.'

Melissa's tone was unfriendly. 'He's away on business.'

'When will he be back?'

'In time for the shareholders' meeting, I imagine. He's received notice of it.'

'That's what I wanted to have a word with him about.'

'Well, I'm afraid you can't. He's travelling around for the next few days and he didn't leave me a number to ring.'

Nicola frowned. 'When did he leave?'

'Thursday morning.'

'Surely he'll ring you sometime?'

'He might,' Melissa drawled. 'And then again, he might not.'

Nicola bit her lip. 'If he does phone, please tell him I need to speak to him urgently.'

'Oh, I will, Nicola. I will.' She spoke with exaggerated earnestness.

Nicola put down the phone with a feeling of anxiety. It was uncharacteristic of her father to disappear into the blue like this.

At the other end of the line Melissa Richmond replaced the handset and smiled mockingly. So, little Nicky was beginning to worry about Daddy's support at the meeting, was she? Good.

Melissa wrapped her arms round her shoulders and hugged herself. She'd waited a long time for this and she was going to enjoy the pleasure of it to the full.

CHAPTER 8

Over the weekend Millson's team methodically visited the five hundred addresses of the male members of the library scattered across the area covered by Mobile Library 3. On Monday morning the team gathered at the Incident Room and gave their reports.

About four hundred of the inquiries had proved negative. The men concerned didn't know Janet West, or had only glimpsed her in the coach occasionally. At thirty of the addresses the men were not at home and would have to be followed up later. Of the remainder who were interviewed, some sixty men admitted Janet had visited them in their homes. The number surprised Millson. Janet West's Samaritan services were more extensive than he'd realized. These men in particular had seemed upset by her death. One had cried. 'Like he'd lost a wife,' a woman constable explained.

A few of them had commented on Janet West's voice. 'Melodious,' said one. 'Kind of breathy,' said another.

After the debriefing Millson sat in his office gloomily smoking a cigarette. The extensive inquiries hadn't produced the information he was seeking. No one knew of any manfriend or had suggested who Janet West might have met in Tanniford on Wednesday evening.

Millson's gloom was made worse by a rift with his daughter earlier that morning. Yesterday evening Dena had returned from her mother's in a bad mood. Recently, his ex-wife had had a baby boy and on Saturday evening Dena had baby-sitted while Jean and her husband went to the cinema. It had not been a happy experience.

'That baby is the pits, Dad!' Dena let loose the moment Millson met her at the station. 'He howled the whole evening and pooed all over his cot. It was *disgusting*. I had to change him. I'm not going there ever again!'

It was Millson's understanding that girls of Dena's age took naturally to babies and he thought there was another reason for her violent reaction. He mentioned it next morning as he met her emerging from the bathroom in her vest and school pants.

'Perhaps you're jealous of your half-brother,' he said.

She stopped dead, gave him a withering look and stalked past him without answering. She burnt his toast at breakfast and when he dropped her off at the school gates she didn't give him the usual peck on the cheek. He knew then he was right, but it was no consolation.

Millson put out his cigarette and picked up the index cards Scobie had separated from the rest when he collected them in from the teams. They were the cards of men who'd been absent from their address. Thumbing through them, Millson paused at one for a Philip Richmond, giving an address in Findlesham.

He rose and opened his door into the operations room. Scobie was sifting through reports.

'Is Philip Richmond any relation to Nicola Richmond?' Millson asked him.

'He's her father. Has a young wife . . . nearly the same age as his daughter.'

'How d'you know?'

'Miss Richmond told me herself on Saturday.'

'Ah yes, she asked to see me, didn't she? What did she want?'

Scobie had been waiting for the right moment to put forward Nicola's plea for a police guard. This was not it, but he had no choice now. He explained Nicola's request and the reason for it.

'We're not in the private security business,' Millson said.

'It would only be for a few days until the launch.'

Millson scowled at him. 'What did she do? Bat her eye-lashes at you?'

'It doesn't seem much to ask,' Scobie muttered, 'and there could be a link with the murder. Janet West might have stumbled across this intruder doing his mischief and he clobbered her to prevent her talking. Well, it's not beyond the realms of possibility.'

Millson said impatiently, 'It doesn't fit the facts. The woman met a man that evening and had sex with him. Her appointment diary is missing—which suggests it contains his name—and the man hasn't come forward. Now, until he does—and clears himself—he's our prime suspect. *He's* the most likely man to have killed her. Not some hypothetical saboteur!' He went back into his room.

A few minutes later Scobie put his head round the door. 'About Philip Richmond. I've been looking through the reports. The DC who called at Richmond's address reported that his wife couldn't confirm he was home Wednesday night. What's more, he left home unexpectedly Thursday morning and she doesn't seem to know when he'll be back.'

'Doesn't she now?' Millson rubbed his chin. 'I think we'd better ask Mrs Richmond one or two questions.'

The search of the riverbed for the murder weapon had been extended downriver beyond the scout barge. Police divers worked their way along, laying out on the bank the daily collection of old boots, bicycle frames and other oddments as they went. Among today's finds was a plastic bag containing a girl guide uniform.

The modern detached house at Findlesham, with its integral double garage, was in a row of six similar houses on the edge of the village. Estate agents called them 'town houses', although they were now a common sight in rural areas and nowhere to be found in towns.

Findlesham stood on a hill on the opposite side of the river from Tanniford. A road led down the hill from the village and across marshland to end abruptly at the water's edge where, in bygone days, a rowing-boat had ferried people across the river to Tanniford.

'The builders tried to put a quart into a pint pot,' Millson commented, pointing to the narrow space between the house and its neighbours either side. He'd parked in the road, not attempting to negotiate the narrow drive that curved in a tight semi-circle in front of the house, using space that would have been better devoted to garden. A white Mercedes stood in the double garage.

He yanked the bellhandle at the side of the front door and winced at the sound of electronic chimes from within.

'Mrs Richmond?' he asked when a tall blonde girl in white slacks and a black halter-top opened the door.

'Yes.' Her tone was curt.

'Detective Chief Inspector Millson and Detective-Sergeant Scobie, Essex CID. We're making inquiries in connection with the murder of Janet West. May we come in?'

She nodded and led them along the hall and into a lounge where a baby grand in the middle of the room vied for space with an overlarge three-piece suite. Along the wall a Welsh dresser struggled to be seen behind the biggest collection of mugs Millson had ever seen outside of a museum. French windows opened on to a long, narrow garden.

Melissa Richmond sank into an armchair and crossed her legs. Millson and Scobie took opposite ends of the vast settee. The space left between them would have seated a trio of constables.

'I've already spoken to a detective who called here yesterday,' Melissa Richmond said as Scobie opened his notebook.

'That's why we're here,' Millson said. 'You told my officer you couldn't say whether or not your husband was at home Wednesday evening.'

'No, because I spent the evening with an old schoolfriend in Tiptree and didn't get back until after midnight. I don't see why it matters?'

'It matters, Mrs Richmond, because your husband belonged to the mobile library and we're anxious to establish where every man who belonged to that library was at the time of the murder.'

'Oh, I see. Well, all I can tell you is that Philip was here when I left and here when I returned and I've no reason to think he went out while I was away.'

'But he could have done?'

'Well . . . yes.'

'And he left here the next morning?'

'Yes. On business.'

'What sort of business?'

'He's an accountant. He works from home. He has clients all round the country.'

Millson leaned forward on the settee. 'So his departure on Thursday morning had been planned beforehand?'

She hesitated. 'Well . . . no. But Philip's like that. Unorganized. He collects mugs . . . in a big way.' She waved a hand at the obscured Welsh dresser. 'Antique mugs, commemorative mugs, advertising mugs . . . the house is full of them. On shelves, in cabinets . . . *everywhere*. They're like mushrooms growing in the night. Some of them are quite valuable, I believe. Philip said the Cranberry— that little red glass thing on the second shelf—is worth a thousand pounds. He's always adding to the collection. He's probably in some junk shop right now, rummaging for mugs.'

'You think that's what he's doing, do you?'

'Yes, because Thursday morning he told me there were several antique fairs in the North this week and he was going to combine business with pleasure and call on one or two clients on the way.'

'Did he say when he'd be back?'

'No. I don't suppose he'll be more than a week, though.' She opened a box of cigarettes on the table beside her and offered it to Millson and Scobie. When they declined she took one for herself and lit it with a table lighter.

'Does your husband own a car?' Millson asked.

She inhaled and blew out smoke. 'Yes. We both do.'

'And did he take the car?'

'No, he went by train. I drove him to the station. He was going to Liverpool Street and catching an Intercity to Newcastle or somewhere.'

At that moment a sturdily-built man with dark hair, wearing an open-necked shirt and jeans, came in through the French windows. 'Missy, when are you—?' He stopped on seeing Millson and Scobie.

Melissa Richmond jumped to her feet. 'These police officers are investigating that woman's murder, Tom. My husband belonged to her library and they want to interview him.'

Millson detected an emphasis in the way she imparted the information, as though she was stressing something to him.

'Tom Lowery does our garden,' she explained, turning to Millson.

'Lowery?' Scobie looked up at the man. 'Aren't you the other security guard at the shipyard?'

'Yeh, that's me.'

'He does the garden in his time off,' Melissa said quickly. She waved a dismissive hand at Lowery. 'I'll speak to you later, Tom.'

He nodded and stepped out through the French windows. Melissa sat down again.

'Did Janet West ever bring books to your husband when the library was in Findlesham?' Millson asked.

'Not that I know of. What day is it here?'

'Wednesday,' Scobie informed her. 'Findlesham is the last call on Wednesday afternoon.'

'I go to see my mother in Chelmsford on Wednesday afternoons, so I wouldn't know,' Melissa Richmond said.

'We'd very much like to speak to your husband, Mrs Richmond,' Millson said. 'Is there some way we can get in touch with him?'

'I'm afraid not,' she said.

'You mean you've no idea where he is?'

'Not exactly, no. I told you, he's up North somewhere.'

'What if there's an emergency and you need him urgently?' Scobie asked.

She raised an eyebrow. 'I can't imagine myself needing Philip urgently. And if I did for some reason . . .' She shrugged. 'Well . . . it would be just too bad.'

Scobie persisted. 'Is it possible he'll phone you?'

She compressed her lips. 'He might, but I doubt it. Surely, you can wait until he comes back to speak to him? He can't possibly know anything about that woman's death.' Her expression suddenly altered. 'Can he?'

'We have no reason to think so at the moment,' Millson said, 'but we do need to eliminate him from our inquiries. So if he does phone you, perhaps you'll ask him to contact us urgently.'

Her expression had become vacant as though her attention had drifted elsewhere. 'Er—yes. Yes, I'll tell him.'

'Fat lot of help she was,' Millson complained, clipping on his seat-belt. 'Her husband belongs to the library, he hasn't an alibi, he unexpectedly leaves home the morning after the murder and she doesn't know where he is. Great!'

He started the car and slammed it into gear. 'Well, I'm hanged if I'm waiting until he decides to return. Let's see if his daughter has a better idea where he is.'

The sergeant in charge of the diving operations looked briefly at the guide uniform and detailed a constable to take it to the Incident Room. From there, as a matter of routine, it was sent away for forensic examination.

CHAPTER 9

Nicola Richmond greeted them with a friendly smile and Scobie realized she thought they had come to discuss police protection for the yard. Behind Millson's back he shook his head warningly and her smile died.

'I was wondering if you could tell me where your father is, Miss Richmond,' said Millson. 'We've just come from your stepmother and she doesn't seem to know where he is, or to be able to contact him.'

'Why do you want him?' she asked.

'He belonged to the mobile library and we're interviewing all the men who belonged to it in order to eliminate them from our inquiries. Can you help us?'

'I'm afraid not. I don't know where he is either. I badly need to speak to him myself. There's an important shareholders' meeting soon and I want to be sure he'll be there.'

'Does he often go off like this without telling anyone where he's going?' Millson asked.

'Not to my knowledge.'

'So this sudden departure was unusual, would you say?'

'Yes, very.'

'Did he have any lady friends?' Millson caught Nicola's frown of disapproval and added, 'This is a murder inquiry and I have to ask these questions, Miss Richmond.'

'Yes, I understand.' Her frown turned to a wry smile. 'You think he's gone off with some woman, do you? I don't know of anyone, but it wouldn't surprise me. His marriage to Melissa was a ghastly mistake.'

No, that isn't what the Chief Inspector thinks, Scobie would have liked to tell her. He suspects Janet West might be the lady friend. And you've just strengthened that suspicion. It troubled Scobie that all Nicola's answers to

Millson's questions were bound to have increased his suspicions of her father.

'Well, thank you for your time,' Millson said, turning to leave.

'What about my request for a police guard, Chief Inspector?'

'I'm afraid I can't help you there, Miss Richmond. It's not our job,' Millson said. 'I'm sorry.'

She turned down her mouth. 'I suppose I'll have to consider guard dogs, then. Some of the men own Dobermans and Pit Bulls.'

Millson's eyebrows rose. 'There's a public right of way through the yard. I assume you're aware of the Dangerous Dogs Act?'

'Well, perhaps you'd prefer me to patrol the yard myself with a shotgun. I have one, you know,' she said provocatively. 'The yard is private property and I have a permit to shoot pests on my own land.'

'It would be very unwise to discharge a firearm in the shipyard in the dark.'

'But not unlawful.'

Scobie saw Millson containing himself with difficulty and, fearful he might explode, he said, 'I'm sure you wouldn't really shoot an intruder if you caught him.'

'Perhaps not.' She glanced up at the portrait of Bertram Richmond. 'My grandfather was a naval officer. He would have hanged the man by the neck from the nearest yard arm. I think I'd hang him up by his testicles. Would that be GBH or malicious wounding, Chief Inspector?'

'That isn't funny,' Millson said severely.

'I didn't mean it to be,' she said lightly.

'She was trying to wind me up,' Millson snarled, stamping down the stairs from Nicola Richmond's office. 'Because I wouldn't do what she wanted.'

'She was upset,' Scobie said. 'She cares passionately

about the yard and she's desperate to make the launch date. You have to see it from her point of view, George.'

Millson gave him a searching look. 'Seems to me you've taken quite a shine to little Miss Richmond, Norris.' His annoyance evaporated in a grin. 'You're right. She's got a tough job. I'll try to keep my hair on in future.'

WDC Tracey Bennett left the Incident Room that afternoon equipped with a street map of Tanniford and the list of names and addresses of the twelve scouts she had been given the task of interviewing by Sergeant Scobie. She was an organized young policewoman. She intended to mark each address on the map and draw lines showing each boy's route home from the scout barge and the time he left there and the time he arrived home.

In the evening, Millson made peace with Dena when he arrived home and was rewarded with a hug and a kiss. After she'd gone to bed, he sat with a large whisky, reflecting on his team's reports on the weekend interviews.

'Made an appointment when they wanted the Book Lady to call . . .' 'She called regularly once a week . . .' 'This old gent said her voice gave him a lift . . . made him rampant . . .'

At some addresses Janet stayed a few minutes, at others twenty minutes or half an hour. Some men she read to, some she didn't. Some visits were weekly, some fortnightly . . . monthly . . . any old time.

Millson sighed. The picture was confused, with no pattern to it, and despite the weekend inquiries, Janet West was eluding him. He took a mouthful of the malt whisky, swilling it around his tongue and savouring the flavour. A policeman should know his murder victim better than this.

In bed that night he dreamed of Janet West. Not as a cold corpse on the grass beside the river, but as a warm-blooded woman with attractive legs and a sensuous voice. In the dream, she was sitting at his dining-table reading to him from a volume of the Encyclopædia Britannica. The words issuing from her lips gave exquisite pleasure as they flowed over him.

The scene changed and she stood in the doorway of a huge yellow coach in a ballooning red dress with layers of black underskirts. A multitude of old men appeared as she descended the steps of the coach. They rushed towards her waving skinny arms excitedly. As the first man reached her and began clawing at her skirts with veined, liver-spotted hands, the dream dissolved.

The next morning Millson decided to look over Janet West's house again. Last night's dream and the suspicion he knew less than he should about the dead woman had spurred him into learning more about her.

He phoned Scobie from home and told him to collect the keys and meet him at Colchester police station.

Looking through the windscreen as he parked, Millson experienced a sensation of *déjà vu*. Laura Stebbing was at the front door of the house as she'd been last Thursday, except that today she was carrying a large suitcase. He glanced up and down the street. There was no sign of the yellow library coach.

'No, wait!' He restrained Scobie as he was about to open the car door. 'Let's see what she does.'

They watched Laura Stebbing take a key from her coat pocket. With a furtive glance over her shoulder, she unlocked the door and entered the house.

'Right!' Millson jumped from the car.

She was still in the hall when Scobie opened the door with Janet West's own key and stepped inside followed by Millson. The fright on her face changed to guilt when she saw who they were.

'What are you doing here, Mrs Stebbing?' Millson asked sternly.

'Um . . . well . . .' She recovered herself and said, 'The library doesn't operate on Mondays, you see. I usually spend it in the office, but today I thought I'd pop in and empty Janet's fridge. The food will go off if it's left any longer.'

'How do you come to have a key?'

'I've always had a key. Janet liked me to have one.'

Millson pointed to the suitcase on the floor beside her. 'And what's that for?'

'Oh . . . that.' She looked down at the case as though it didn't belong to her. 'I was going to sort through Janet's clothes while I was here and see what fitted me.'

'And you were going to take them away?'

'Er—yes. The solicitor said it would be all right.'

'What solicitor?' Scobie asked.

'Janet's. She left everything to me in her will . . . the house . . . money . . . everything. All her worldly goods.' She gave a sudden, excited laugh. 'Like in the old marriage service, you know. "With all my worldly goods I thee endow."' She waved an arm in the air. 'It's mine . . . all mine.' Her eyes rolled, then steadied and fastened on Millson. 'This is *my* house now,' she said in the voice of a child snatching away another child's possession.

'Not until the solicitor has obtained probate,' Millson warned. 'Until then I'd advise you to stay out of the property. And certainly you mustn't remove anything from it.'

She glowered at him and Millson thought she was going to argue the point. Instead, she uttered an exaggerated sigh and picked up the suitcase.

'Oh, very well then,' she said. 'I'll go.'

She pushed past them and out of the door, closing it noisily behind her.

Millson made a face and shrugged. 'We'll start in here,' he said, opening the sitting-room door.

Searching the bureau desk, Millson found a building society deposit book among the bills and receipts in one of the compartments. Opening it, he glanced at the total on the last page of entries and let out a whistle of surprise.

'There's over fifty thousand pounds in here,' he said, passing the book to Scobie. 'How does a library assistant accumulate that amount of money?'

Scobie was scanning the entries. 'Frequent deposits—almost daily—varying between twenty and a hundred pounds.' He looked up. 'Blackmail?'

'Could be. And possibly a motive for murder.'

'By a victim, you mean?'

'I was thinking more of Mrs Stebbing,' Millson said. 'That is, assuming she knew about Janet's will and the amount of money involved. On top of which there's the house and furniture and any other assets.' He took the deposit book from Scobie and replaced it in the desk. 'Let's take a look upstairs.'

The bedroom was still fragrant with scent, more pervasive now the room had been shut up for a while. The bouquet stirred bitter-sweet memories in George Millson, memories of a childhood sweetheart . . . her heady perfume . . . the nervous thrill of a first kiss.

He made for a chest of drawers. Behind him Scobie opened the doors of a fitted wardrobe that extended the length of the wall.

Millson pulled out the top drawer of the chest and rifled through the assortment of briefs and brassieres with unaccustomed embarrassment. The dream had brought Janet West alive for him, changed her from murder victim to living woman, and he was invading her privacy. A psychiatrist would have an explanation for it, he supposed.

The middle drawer contained stockings, tights and suspender belts. He opened the bottom drawer.

For a moment he gazed in perplexity at the voluminous elastic-legged knickers in sombre shades of blue, green, khaki and black. Surely Janet West didn't wear these?

He stood, bemused, filtering stray thoughts from the past
. . . *Passion-killers* . . . *Twilights* . . . *Blackouts* . . . his father
and uncle reminiscing over the War . . . about WAAFS
who wore Twilights in summer and Blackouts in winter.
The penny dropped for Millson. These garments—some of
them at any rate—were Service issue underwear.

His disjointed thoughts began making connections. He
strode to the wardrobe where Scobie was closing the doors.
'Nothing in here,' Scobie said.

Millson elbowed him aside and pulled the doors open
again. He yanked the hanging dresses and skirts to one end
of the brass rail. At the other end of the long rail, deep in
the cupboard, he saw uniforms and pulled them towards
him. There were Women's Service uniforms, a traffic war-
den's, a nurse's outfit, gymslips . . .

Watched by an astonished Scobie, he lifted an Air Force
blue jacket and skirt from their hanger and laid them on
the bed.

'Janet West didn't just read naughty stories, Norris. She
lived out fantasies too—for a fee. That's where those
deposits in the building society came from.'

'Laura Stebbing *must* have known what was going on,'
Scobie said.

'Too right she did,' Millson agreed. 'And that's why she
had that big suitcase with her today. She wasn't interested
in the dresses and skirts—they wouldn't have fitted her.
Janet was size fourteen and Laura Stebbing is an eighteen
at least. The suitcase was to cart this lot away in. To remove
the evidence. Come on, Norris. I can't wait to hear what
she has to say.'

CHAPTER 10

The expression of surprise on Laura Stebbing's face turned to resignation when she opened the door of her bungalow at Weeley and saw Millson and Scobie for the second time that day. She glanced over her shoulder.

'My husband's home having his lunch. Can you come back later?'

'No,' Millson said firmly, 'I'd like the answers to some questions and I'd like them *now*, Mrs Stebbing. There's no reason to involve your husband.'

'You'd better tell him that yourself,' she muttered as a thick-set man appeared behind her, jaws champing. His brown hair was greasy and he had thin lips.

'What's all this, then?' The man's tone was truculent. 'Who are you people?'

'Essex CID. I'm Detective Chief Inspector Millson and this is Detective-Sergeant Scobie,' Millson told him curtly. 'I'm conducting a murder investigation and I'd like to ask your wife some questions. May we come in?'

Stebbing gave a performance of considering the request before answering, 'Yes, all right.'

Millson and Scobie followed Laura Stebbing into the front room. 'Hold on,' her husband said as Scobie went to shut the door on him. 'I want to be in on this.'

Laura Stebbing gave Millson a look of 'I told you so'.

'This doesn't concern you, Mr Stebbing,' Millson said.

'Oh yes it does. She's my wife.' Stebbing pushed past Scobie.

Millson kept his temper. 'We can question your wife here or she can accompany us to the nearest police station and be questioned there. Myself, I'd prefer to do it here. So, unless you want my sergeant to arrest you for obstructing a police officer in the execution of his duties, I suggest you leave us.'

For an instant, Ronald Stebbing's eyes blazed with anger. Then he slouched from the room, slamming the door behind him. Scobie heard Laura Stebbing sigh with relief.

They took seats. Millson, certain that Laura Stebbing realized the reason for their visit, decided to make an indirect approach. Instead of starting with a stern warning over having withheld information, he brought out his cigarettes and offered them to her.

Her hand rose . . . hovered in the air . . . and fell. 'Go on,' he said encouragingly, pushing the packet at her.

'Oh, all right, I will,' she said. 'Thanks.' With a nervous glance at the door she took one.

As he lit it for her she said with a giggle, 'I hardly ever do, you know, but I did sometimes have one with Janet when we were on the road.'

He lit his own cigarette. 'Did you know she had made that will leaving everything to you?'

She hesitated. 'No. Though sometimes she joked about having no one else to leave her money to. I was thunderstruck. It was very generous of her, bless her heart.'

'Did the solicitor tell you how *much* she left?'

She was taking quick puffs at her cigarette like a beginner. 'Goodness me, no! I'm not sure if he knows himself yet.' She lowered her voice to a whisper, 'You won't tell my husband about Janet's will, will you?'

Millson shook his head and she continued, still whispering, 'I'm going to leave him, you see. He'd kill me if he knew.'

For leaving him? For the money she'd inherit? Or didn't she mean it literally? Scobie thought she did and remembering the violence in Ronald Stebbing's eyes, he scribbled a note in his book.

Millson was following a different line of thought. Fifty thousand pounds and a house were worth killing for, especially if you were planning to escape from an odious husband.

'Just for the record, Mrs Stebbing,' he asked, 'do you mind telling us where you were last Wednesday evening?'

'I was here at home . . . watching TV.'

'With your husband?'

'No, he was out. Wednesday night is his darts night.'

A thought occurred to Millson. He asked casually, 'Did your husband know Janet?'

'Only as someone I worked with. They never met.'

'And what does he do for a living?'

'He used to work at the shipyard in Tanniford. Now he's in business for himself. He's a painter and decorator.'

Millson moved on to the main purpose of his visit. 'You were very fond of Janet, weren't you?' His voice was heavy with sympathy.

'Oh yes,' she breathed, 'I loved her.'

She took several more puffs at her cigarette, then reached across him and stubbed the end in an ashtray. He glanced at the crumpled remnant. It was only half-smoked.

'We . . .' her mouth trembled with emotion, 'we were going away together, you know. Away . . .' she tossed her head in the direction of the door, 'away from *him*. And now . . .' she gave a sob, 'now she's gone.'

'I know . . . I know.'

The warmth and compassion in Millson's voice made Scobie look up from his notebook. He watched in surprise as Millson leaned forward and grasped Laura Stebbing's hand.

'Laura . . . I want you to tell us everything you can about your friend, Janet. About the men she read to . . . about the uniforms in her wardrobe . . . everything. There's nothing to be afraid of. We just want to catch her murderer. And I know that's what you want too.'

In her white fluffy jumper she sat bright-eyed and motionless like a mesmerized Angora rabbit. Holding her eyes with his own, Millson said softly, 'Shall we start with the library, Laura, and the old gentlemen she read to? Janet didn't just read to them, did she?'

Laura Stebbing sagged in her chair. 'Yes, all right. It's been awful keeping it to myself.' She gave a long sigh like someone slipping into a trance. 'Janet liked older men, you see, I mean *really* liked them—especially men on their own . . . men who were widowed, separated, divorced or whatever.'

George Millson was in the 'divorced or whatever' category, Scobie thought. He wasn't old, of course, but he'd still be in that category when he was. Unless he remarried. And he showed no sign of doing that.

Laura Stebbing went on. 'Many of these men are lonely. East Anglia has the highest suicide rate in the country among elderly men and Janet looked upon what she did as a kind of social service. She gave them warmth and affection . . . a bit of a cuddle and squeeze.' Her face turned away from him. 'You know.'

'But with some it went further, didn't it?' Millson prompted. 'And she charged them.'

'Oh yes. Not a lot, though. It depended on what they could afford. She was fair like that. Usually it was only a fiver or a tenner at the most.'

'How many—um—clients did she have?' Millson asked.

'Only a few to start with. Then it grew and grew. Now there must be . . .' She closed her eyes, considering. 'Let's see . . . thirty villages . . . forty-five stops . . . one or two at each stop . . .' Her eyes opened. 'I suppose there are fifty or sixty. She didn't visit them every week, of course. She used to make four or five calls a day—say twenty a week.'

'How did she fit all this in with the timetable and run the library as well?'

Laura Stebbing gave a slight smile. 'I told you before, Chief Inspector, it doesn't need two to operate the library most of the time, especially if one of us is willing to work a little harder. And Janet was always careful not to make us late.'

Millson ground his cigarette out in the ashtray. 'Tell me about the uniforms we found in her wardrobe—evidence you intended to remove, I think.'

'Only to protect Janet's good name. She wasn't a bad person. She was good . . . kind . . .' She broke off and ferreted in her skirt pocket for a handkerchief. 'The papers would sensationalize everything . . . print lies about her and make her out to be something she wasn't . . .' She sniffed and blew her nose. 'And now it will all come out, I suppose.'

'Not if we can help it,' Millson assured her firmly.

'Oh, good.' She brightened. 'Well, the uniforms were what you'd call a more professional part of her service, for men who wanted their fantasies brought to life and could afford her fee of fifty pounds. These were evening and week-end appointments and always at their place, not hers. She used to take the outfit with her in the car and change when she got there. Very good at it, she was too. She gave me a demonstration once. It was very authentic.'

'And how many of these evening and weekend appointments would she have?'

'I think she did six or seven a week.'

Scobie, busily recording Laura's flood of information, did a quick calculation. Together with her daytime calls, Janet West had been making over five hundred pounds a week. The figure tallied with the payments into her building society account.

As though echoing his thoughts, Laura Stebbing said, 'She was doing very well. She was saving up, you see . . . for both of us. We were going to emigrate—we'd already started making plans. She had it all worked out. And now . . .' She stifled a sob. 'It's all gone . . . all the fun . . . all our hopes . . .'

Millson leaned forward and patted her hand. She looked

up at him miserably. 'I shall still go away . . . leave him,' she said. 'That's what Janet would have wanted me to do. We were almost there, you know. Another month or two, Janet said.' Laura Stebbing stopped, her eyes glistening. 'And then some wicked mugger went and killed her.'

'It wasn't a mugger,' Millson said. 'It was someone who wanted to make it *look* like a mugging. I think the man she met was a client and she was meeting him for sex.'

Laura Stebbing shook her head vigorously. 'No. Janet didn't allow sex. At least—' she looked embarrassed—'not real sex. Besides, an evening appointment would have been for dressing-up and you didn't find a uniform in her car, did you?'

Millson shook his head. 'Maybe he didn't belong to the library.'

'Janet wouldn't go with anyone who didn't. She said if they joined the library she knew who they were and had some idea what they were like. More importantly, she knew where they lived. She was very, very careful.'

'In that case,' Millson said a shade impatiently, 'he has to be a man she didn't tell you about.'

She gave him a scornful look, making it clear she didn't believe her friend Janet would keep a thing like that from her.

Millson regarded her thoughtfully. Perhaps she was right. The rest of the men belonging to the library, the ones who'd been absent from their addresses over the weekend, had now been interviewed and accounted for. Except Philip Richmond.

'Laura, when we spoke before you told me you knew the names of some of the men Janet visited. Was one of them a Philip Richmond?'

She smiled slightly. 'I knew them by the stops. Can you tell me which stop he lived at.'

'Findlesham.'

'Ah yes. There was a Philip she called on there some-times. He lived in one of those big modern houses.'

Scobie, writing down Laura Stebbing's response, knew without looking up that Millson's face wore a satisfied expression at this further justification of his suspicions of Nicola's father.

Millson stood up. 'Thank you, Laura. You've been very helpful . . . very helpful indeed.'

She jumped up and laid a hand on his arm. 'What shall I do about the funeral? People are asking when it will be and I don't know what to say.'

Millson pursed his lips. After some recent miscarriages of justice, where evidence had come to light that had been denied to the defence at the time, there was an increasing tendency to hang on to a body until someone was charged and brought to trial so that the defence could conduct its own forensic examination. It was not something he wanted to elaborate upon to Janet West's loving friend.

'The Coroner's Office will let you know when they can release the body,' he said. Even that brought moisture to Laura Stebbing's eyes.

At the door he paused. Tomorrow it would be a week since the murder and he still had no idea where Janet West went or what she did after she parked her car outside the shipyard that night. Who better than her close friend to imitate her actions?

'Laura, would you be willing to take part in a recon-struction?'

'Yes, I'll do anything to help.'

'Thanks. We'll send a car for you tomorrow evening.'

'Go and see Philip Richmond's wife first thing in the morn-ing,' Millson instructed Scobie as they drove away. 'Find out what train he caught and where these antique fairs are. She must have some idea. And ask her for a list of his business contacts.'

'You've settled on him as a suspect then?'

Millson said patiently, 'He belonged to the library, we've just established Janet West used to visit him, he left in a hurry the morning after the murder and now no one knows where he is. Of course he's a suspect!'

'She might have been simply delivering books to him— she did that for some people. And he doesn't fit the picture of her other clients,' Scobie argued. 'He's only fifty and he doesn't live on his own.'

'No, but his wife's at her mother's on Wednesday after-noons when the library calls. She said so herself.'

'Then why meet Janet in Tanniford in the evening?'

'Because it's the ideal place for him to spend more time with her,' Millson said. 'He knows the shipyard—he must do, his daughter owns it—and he probably has a key to one of the offices.'

'Why kill her, though?'

'That's what we have to find out. Perhaps she tried to blackmail him—threatened to tell his wife.'

'I don't buy that,' Scobie said. 'She was pulling in over five hundred pounds a week and Laura Stebbing said she'd nearly reached her target.'

Millson rounded the roundabout on to the A133 to Col-chester and they drove in silence for a while.

As they approached Frating, Scobie asked, 'You don't think Laura Stebbing was lying and *did* know about the will? If she discovered what a pot of gold Janet was sitting on so she might have decided to knock her on the head and take it all for herself. Those blows to the head could have been delivered by a woman.'

Millson nodded. 'I considered the possibility before I questioned her. Having listened to her, though, it's obvious she was deeply attached to Janet. No, she didn't kill her friend.'

'What about the husband, then? He's a real nasty piece of work. Suppose he'd found out Janet was leaving Laura her money? He could have murdered her so's Laura inherited and then force Laura to hand it over to him.'

'Way out, Norris, too far-fetched.' Millson lifted his eyes briefly from the road to Scobie. 'You're just trying to divert me from Philip Richmond because you've fallen for his daughter.'

Scobie opened his mouth to protest and caught the slight grin on George Millson's face just in time.

'See if you can pick up one or two of his hairs while you're quizzing Melissa Richmond,' Millson said.

'Hairs?' Scobie gaped at him.

'Yes. You know, Norris—the stuff that keeps your head warm. You find them on clothes . . . hairbrushes . . . combs . . . Shouldn't be too difficult for you.'

'What do you want them for?'

'There were hairs on Janet West's clothes that weren't her own. I want to see if they match Philip Richmond's.'

CHAPTER 11

Scobie called early on Melissa Richmond to be sure of catching her at home. He need not have worried. She was still in bed and came to the door in black silk pyjamas and white mules.

'I have a lie-in on Wednesdays,' she explained, 'usually until eleven when I go off to see my mother.'

She led him down the hall and into the kitchen, passing a row of hanging coats on the way but making no attempt to take one to cover herself with. Scobie saw a man's raincoat among the coats and wished he'd brought an accomplice with him who could have scoured it for hairs while he questioned Melissa in the kitchen.

'Would you like some coffee?' She perched on a high stool and crossed her legs.

'Not now, thanks. Later, perhaps.' Scobie pulled out his notebook. 'The Chief Inspector is anxious to locate your husband as soon as possible Could you tell me what train he caught last Thursday?'

'The eight-thirty from Colchester North. As I told you, I drove him to the station myself.'

'Did you see him actually board the train?'

She looked amused. 'I didn't go on to the platform with him and kiss him goodbye, if that's what you mean. But I'm sure he caught it all right.'

Scobie glanced at his notes. 'You said he was going down to London to catch the Intercity to Newcastle.'

'I said I *thought* that was what he was doing,' she corrected.

'Well, could you let me have the addresses of his clients and give me some idea where those antique fairs you mentioned might be, please?'

'My, what a lot of things you want to know, Sergeant,' she said teasingly. 'I think you'll find everything you want in his study. It's through here.'

He followed her across the hall and into a small room furnished with a desk and chair. A PC stood on a table next to a photocopier.

'He kept most of his information on computer, but there's a printout of his clients somewhere.' She ferreted among some papers. 'Here it is. I'll make you a copy.' She switched on the photocopier.

Scobie saw a copy of the *Antique Collector*, lying on the window-sill and picked it up.

She noticed and said, 'You can take that if you like. I think you'll find one or two sales in there near Newcastle.' She handed him the photocopy. 'By the way, Philip was carrying a very distinctive travelling bag. One of a pair.'

'Can you describe it, please?'

'Better still, I'll show you. Come with me.'

She took hold of his hand and led him into the hall and up the stairs. The intimate way she clasped his hand disturbed him. That, and the whisper of silk on her thighs as they mounted the stairs together.

'We have separate bedrooms,' she explained as she opened a door on the landing. 'This is my husband's.' She still had hold of his hand and drew him across the room to a fitted wardrobe. Releasing him, she opened the door and lifted out a black canvas travelling bag and laid it on the bed. It had the initials P.R. in gilt letters beneath the lock.

'The one he's taken with him is exactly the same as this.'

Scobie looked at it and nodded. He was wondering how he could pluck some hairs from the hairbrush on the dressing-table.

'Are you sure you won't have coffee?' she asked. 'I was just about to make some.'

'Well, in that case . . . yes, please.' He took out his note-book and made a pretence of examining the bag. 'I'd like to jot down a full description of this bag first, though.'

The ruse worked and she said, 'OK, I'll go and put the kettle on, then.' She left the room and he heard her click-clack down the stairs in her mules.

He moved swiftly to the dressing-table and teased several hairs from the brush. Taking a small specimen bag from his pocket he carefully inserted the hairs and replaced it in his pocket. Then he sauntered downstairs and joined Melissa in the kitchen.

She was spooning coffee granules into cups. 'Have you tried his daughter? She might know where he is.'

'Yes. She doesn't.'

'What did you think of my stepdaughter?' A mocking smile hovered around her mouth. Scobie shrugged non-committally, not wanting to be drawn into a discussion of Nicola.

'All efficiency and business.' There was malice in the smile now. 'Not very feminine, is she?'

Scobie completely disagreed, but he didn't intend to debate Nicola's attractiveness with Melissa Richmond. The two were complete opposites. Nicola was slim, dark and petite and her movements were neat and economical. Melissa was a tall, buxom blonde who moved restlessly like a predator. Scobie suspected that bedding with Melissa Richmond would be like being mauled by a lioness.

He swallowed scalding coffee and took his leave. As he left she asked, 'Why are you so keen to find Philip? Has something happened to make him a suspect?'

'We need to eliminate him from our inquiries, Mrs Richmond, that's all.'

'That means he's a suspect until you do, doesn't it?' She sounded interested rather than concerned.

'I suppose you could say that,' Scobie agreed reluctantly. 'Thanks for the coffee.'

'Any time, Sergeant.' Her eyes met his boldly.

*

A few minutes before nine o'clock that Wednesday evening Janet West's Fiat Panda, followed by a police car, was driven into the shipyard car park by Laura Stebbing. As she parked in the position a policewoman was indicating the car had been found a week ago, a police team with a videocamera began recording the reconstruction for later release to the news media.

Laura heaved herself from the driving seat, locked the car and looked around her. After a moment she turned and headed towards the shipyard. She was wearing Janet West's fawn raincoat, which Scobie had borrowed from the exhibits officer and as she approached the group waiting at the entrance, Millson saw that her face was made-up and she was wearing high heels to make herself look more like Janet.

Standing with Millson and Scobie were Leonard Pearson, who'd been on duty the previous Wednesday, Tom Lowery who was on duty tonight, and Nicola Richmond.

'You'd better let Miss Richmond know about the reconstruction,' Millson had told Scobie. 'We may need her cooperation.'

Millson turned to Pearson. 'Where were you at this time, Mr Pearson?'

Pearson glanced at his watch. 'On me rounds, I guess. Not here, anyway.'

'So the entrance was unmanned. Stand away from it then, if you please.'

Laura Stebbing walked through the entrance, ignoring the onlookers as she'd been instructed. 'We're not going to prompt you,' Scobie had told her. 'Try to imagine you're Janet and you're meeting a man. Mr Millson hopes that, knowing her so well, you might be able to anticipate what she would have done.'

Laura had been flattered by their trust and had an affection for the ogre-like Chief Inspector who'd held her hand and whose eyes gave her a funny feeling inside as they gazed into hers. She was determined to do her best to please him and help find Janet's killer.

She walked past the shed at the entrance that served as an office and on into the yard where she stopped and peered about her in the approaching twilight.

Millson cast an eye upwards at the sky. 'Would it have been dark this time last week?' he asked Scobie.

Scobie wrinkled his forehead. 'Well . . . daylight is increasing four and a half minutes a day now—about half an hour a week. Last Wednesday sunrise would have been a quarter of an hour later and sunset a quarter of an hour earlier. So, yes, it would have been dark now.'

'Thank you for the lecture, Norris,' Millson said heavily. 'I only wanted a yes or no.'

In front of Laura Stebbing, the shipyard was already in gloom below the hull of *Vivacity* which dominated the yard and cast its own deeper shadow. To her left, the ground was strewn with assorted offcuts of steelplate. Above, the long arm of a crane poked into the darkening sky. She turned right to the administration block where a light shone over a door on the ground floor.

The spectators followed her as she walked along the administration building and paused by the door. Security lights within glowed through the frosted glass in windows either side of the door.

Further on, past the tall building clad with corrugated sheets, was the tidal dock where the ship would be fitted-out after launching. Beyond it stretched the village riverfront with boats moored along its length as far as the timberyard on the other side of the village.

Earlier in the investigation, Millson had complained, 'If only we knew where Janet West went with this man we'd be a lot further forward, Norris.'

'We've questioned everyone living within two hundred yards of here and drawn blank,' Scobie said. 'I suppose they could have sat in her car.'

'Forensic don't think so.'

Until tonight, Millson hadn't thought of the boats moored along the quay. Boats with cabins and bunks. Cosy . . . private. As he warmed to the idea, however, hoping to see Laura walk on, she turned and tried the door. It was locked.

Millson turned to Pearson. 'Was the door locked Wednesday night?'

Pearson shrugged. 'Far as I know.'

'Where's the key?'

It was Lowery who answered. 'All the keys are on a board in the office at the entrance.'

'Fetch it, please,' Millson ordered.

Lowery hurried away and returned with the key. He unlocked the door and Laura Stebbing opened it and stepped inside. She hesitated at the sight of piles of equipment and ship's chandlery and was about to withdraw when she noticed a stairway and made towards it.

Nicola Richmond tugged Millson's arm. 'Chief Inspector, that leads to my office. It's locked and only I and my secretary have the key.'

'No matter,' he said. 'Let's see what she does.' He followed Laura Stebbing as she ascended the stairs.

She walked slowly along the landing above that was dimly lit by a security bulb. With a doubtful glance at the Chubb lock on Nicola Richmond's door and the one on her secretary's opposite, she continued to another door further along the landing.

Tentatively, she stretched out a hand and tried the handle. The door was unlocked. Opening it, she stepped inside and switched on the light. Millson heard her gasp with surprise and moved quickly forward. Over her shoulder he saw a bed made up with white sheets and pillow cases. His head whipped round. 'What's this?'

Behind him Nicola Richmond said, 'That's a rest room.

We're obliged by law to have one, in case anyone is taken ill. It's never used.'

Millson pushed past Laura Stebbing and stood looking down at the bed. Nicola Richmond joined him. Scobie remained in the doorway with Tom Lowery craning over his shoulder.

Millson's nostrils began twitching. 'D'you mind moving away, Miss Richmond? You're confusing me.'

Staring at him in amazement, she joined Laura Stebbing and Scobie at the door.

'What does he mean, she's confusing him?' Laura whispered to Scobie.

'I haven't the faintest idea,' he said, watching in consternation as Millson bent over the bed and began sniffing the pillow and sheets like a bloodhound.

'Sherlock Holmes is alive and well and living in Colchester,' Nicola Richmond murmured.

'Actually, the Chief Inspector lives in Lexden,' Scobie said as Millson straightened and turned to them with a triumphant expression.

'Janet West's perfume!' he announced. 'It's on the bed.' He came to the door, pushing everyone outside and pulling it closed behind him.

'Post a constable here, Norris. No one's to enter this room until forensic have examined it.'

Laura Stebbing squeaked with a mixture of pain and delight as Millson put an arm round her shoulders and hugged her like a bear. 'Well done, Laura! Well done!' he said.

Pearson, hanging about in the room below, took Lowery aside as he trooped down the stairs with the others.

'What did they find?' he asked anxiously.

'The top man reckons that's where she got laid,' Lowery told him with a leer.

CHAPTER 12

The forensic team worked through the night gathering evidence from the shipyard rest-room and analysing it. The results were telephoned to Millson in the morning. No trace of blood had been found in the room and there were no signs of a struggle. Hairs of three different types had been found on the bed linen and pillow. One matched Janet West's hair and one matched the strands of Philip Richmond's hair sent to the laboratory by Scobie yesterday afternoon. These matched hairs found on Janet West's clothes at the post-mortem.

'Hah!' said Millson in a tone of satisfaction.

'Hang on, Chief Inspector,' said David Croft, the forensic scientist on the other end of the phone. 'There were also hairs on her that matched the third specimen from the rest-room.'

'Damn!' said Millson.

'And there's no way of telling when any of these hairs were deposited on the bed. I can say with certainty that she lay down on it and this is probably how the hairs came to be on her clothing, but what I can't say is which hairs were there before, after, or at the same time as hers. For all we know, they could have been there for ages and she picked them up on her clothes simply by lying down on the bed.'

Millson sighed. Trust Croft to make a meal of the logical possibilities. 'All right, point taken. Can you at least confirm that Richmond had intercourse with her?'

'Not from the microscopic examination of his hair. We'll have to do a DNA comparison with the semen found in her body.'

'How long will that take?' Millson asked.

'DNA profiling takes time and it'll have to be done by the Central Laboratory at Aldermaston. Could take forty-eight hours.'

'Very well. Let me know as soon as you can.' Millson hung up.

He called Scobie into his room and recounted Croft's report. 'Where the heck was Pearson while these two were cavorting in the rest-room, Norris? And how did they walk into the shipyard and enter the rest-room without him knowing? Fetch him down here. He has some explaining to do.'

Leonard Pearson was not at home when Scobie walked up the High Street to Station Road and knocked on his door.

'It's his day off,' his wife said. 'He's on his allotment. You'll find him up by King George's Fields on the other side of the village.'

Scobie decided against walking and returned to the Incident Room and picked up his car. Passing the estate agent's on the corner of Station Road, he averted his head as he'd done several times before to avoid seeing Kathy Benson at her desk.

This time, however, the door suddenly opened and he looked round to find himself gazing into her violet eyes.

'How many more times are you going to pass my window without so much as a look, Norris?' she asked.

'I've been busy,' he muttered. 'I'm working on a murder case.'

'I know that! The whole village knows it! Just because we've put our relationship on hold doesn't mean we can't be polite to each other.'

Polite. Scobie's frustration erupted. 'All right, I'll wave next time I pass. Will that do?'

She flinched at his anger, then turned and ran back inside.

*

When Scobie returned with Leonard Pearson, Millson had a plan of the shipyard on his desk. A dog-eared exercise book lay on top of it. As Pearson sat down Millson picked up the book and waved it at him. 'Don't put much in your log-book, do you?'

'Not unless something happens.' Pearson's tone was surly.

Opening the book, Millson showed him the typewritten sheet pasted inside the front page. 'These are your instructions, right? They list the checks you have to make during the night?'

'Yes.' Pearson's expression had become wary.

Millson handed him the book and pointed to the plan of the shipyard. 'Show me on here what you did and where you went between the time you came on duty last Wednesday night and eleven o'clock.'

Pearson nodded and stared down at the plan. 'I signed on in the office at the entrance here at seven.' He put a grimed forefinger on the spot, then turned the pages of the book and showed Millson a scrawled signature. 'Then I walked round the yard checking there weren't no welding torches or equipment left lying about.' He traced a zigzag route back and forth across the plan. 'That took about a half-hour. I comes back to me office and has a cup of tea and a read of the paper. Then at nine I takes the keys and goes round the buildings and sheds to make sure they's locked and all's well.' His finger hopped among the shaded-in buildings on the plan.

'Do you go inside the buildings?'

'No. I jes' try the doors to see they's locked.'

'You didn't go into the administration block?'

'No.'

'What time was it when you checked the downstairs door there?' Millson asked.

'Can't remember for sure 'cos I bin on duty two or three

times since then. It was me last call . . . so I'd reckon about half nine.'

'And then you returned to your office at the entrance?'

Pearson nodded. He was sweating slightly.

Millson went on, 'We know the murdered woman lay down on the rest-room bed because forensic have identified hairs on the pillow as hers. There were other hairs there too. I believe some of them belong to the man who killed her. Does anyone else have keys to the administration block?'

Pearson shrugged. 'There'll be duplicate keys some-where, I 'spect.'

'Uh-huh.' Millson leaned forward. 'What I find difficult to understand, Mr Pearson, is how this man and woman could walk into the yard, enter the administration block and go up to the rest-room and come out again, without you seeing them.'

Pearson stayed silent and Millson went on, 'Janet West was killed between nine and ten—while you were on your round of the offices.' He stared into Pearson's face. 'This man smashed her head in, put her body in a wheelbarrow and wheeled her across the yard and out on to the riverbank where he dumped it.' His voice rose sharply. 'And while all this was going on *you* heard and saw *nothing*?'

'I can't help it if I didn't see 'em.' There were beads of sweat on Pearson's face.

Millson sat back in his chair and studied him. After a while he said, 'Must be pretty boring, night duty work. What d'you do? In between rounds, I mean. How d'you pass the time?' Do you read books? Play Patience? What?'

Pearson was eyeing him suspiciously. 'I read the paper.'

'All night? Or do you have a little nap, perhaps?'

''Ere! You saying I sleep on the job?' Pearson demanded angrily.

'I wouldn't blame you,' Millson went on. 'And we cer-tainly wouldn't tell anyone. But I need an explanation of

how you missed seeing or hearing anything. If not . . .' He
left the rest of the sentence in the air.

For a time Pearson said nothing. Then he said cautiously,
'I might take a kip now and again.'

'Where?'

'Here and there.'

'In the rest-room?'

'No!' Pearson began to protest. 'I don't—'

Millson cut him short. 'Some of the hairs on the bed
were light brown.' He gazed pointedly at Pearson's hair.
'Would you rather be accused of murder?'

'No, 'course not!' Pearson looked frightened. Then his
face changed and a crafty expression came into his eyes.
'OK, I do have a sleep in the rest-room sometimes—not
for long, mind. Wouldn't be surprised if Tom Lowery ain't
done so too. An' I was in there last Wednesday. It must've
bin soon after they left an' that's why I didn't see nor hear
nothing of the murder.' There was an expression of relief
on his face now.

Millson was puzzled by the change in Pearson and wondered if he was missing something. 'I take it you've no
objection to supplying a sample of your hair?'

The relief fled from Pearson's face and his eyes narrowed.
'Whaffor?'

'For the purposes of elimination.'

'Oh. OK then.'

Millson nodded to Scobie. Scobie leaned across the table
and tweaked out a strand of Pearson's hair between thumb
and forefinger. He opened a drawer in the table, took out
an envelope and put the hair into it. He stuck down the
envelope and wrote Pearson's name on it.

'Thank you, Mr Pearson,' Millson said. 'That's all for
now.'

Pearson left and Millson turned to Scobie. 'Philip Richmond probably has a key to the admin block and took Janet
up to the rest-room while Pearson was on his rounds the

other side of the yard. Then later, after they'd left, Pearson went to the rest-room for a sleep and was in there while Richmond was outside in the yard murdering Janet and disposing of her body.'

'That's only speculation,' Scobie protested, unhappy with the prospect of Nicola being the daughter of a killer.

'Finding Richmond's hairs on the bed and on her clothes is good enough for me, Norris. He's all but sewn up,' Millson said confidently. 'We'll launch a full-scale hunt for him after we've questioned his wife again.'

Melissa Richmond was wearing a shirtwaister dress in blue gingham that made her look like a schoolgirl.

'Another visit? So soon?' Her smile as she opened the door was aimed at Scobie.

'No, I haven't heard from my husband,' she said in response to a question from Millson as they followed her into the lounge and took seats on the long settee again. 'But he's bound to return for the shareholders' meeting next Wednesday.'

'Suppose he doesn't?' Scobie asked. Since yesterday afternoon the Incident Room staff had phoned round Philip Richmond's list of clients. He had not called on any of them.

She smiled maliciously. 'Then dear Nicola will lose her precious shipyard.'

'Why?' Scobie asked in alarm.

'Because the meeting is going to vote on a proposal to sell the yard to a developer for a housing estate. Nicola only holds forty per cent of the shares and if Philip doesn't show up and support her with his fifteen per cent she'll be outvoted and the yard will be sold.'

Millson took up the questioning. 'Mrs Richmond, were you aware of a relationship between your husband and the dead woman, Janet West?'

'Relationship?' She looked surprised. 'What kind of relationship?'

'We have reason to believe it was an intimate one.'

'You mean he was screwing her?' An amused smile spread over Melissa Richmond's face. 'No, I didn't know that. Naughty old Philip.'

'You don't seem very concerned,' Millson said.

'I'm not. My husband is a much older than me, Chief Inspector. If he's found someone else to service his needs, that's fine by me.' She read the question in Millson's eyes. 'Yes, that's right. I don't sleep with him.'

'I see. So, would he have minded if you found out about him and Janet West?'

She smiled faintly. 'Oh . . . probably. He'd be full of guilt, I expect.' Her mouth twisted. 'He'd be more upset if Nicola got to hear of it, of course.'

'His daughter? Why?'

'He'd be afraid of losing her respect. Not that she has much respect for him—she treats him like a little boy. She has no love for me, but she certainly wouldn't approve of him committing adultery.' Melissa laughed unpleasantly. 'She'd probably cut off his dividends or something.'

'So if Janet West had threatened to expose the relationship,' Millson began, 'he'd—'

'Philip would do his nut,' Melissa said. Her blonde eyebrows came together in a frown. 'You believe Philip killed this woman, don't you?' There was no dismay in her voice, only curiosity.

'Until I can speak to your husband I can't come to any conclusion about that,' Millson said evasively. 'He hasn't visited any of the addresses you gave Sergeant Scobie yesterday, so I'm going to make a public appeal for him to contact us. It would help if you could give us a description of him and the clothes he was wearing.'

She looked startled. 'Yes, OK.' She lay back in the armchair and half-closed her eyes. 'He's fifty . . . about five

foot six . . . dark hair turning grey at the sides . . . and
wears glasses. Now, what did he have on?' She put a finger
to her lips in concentration. 'Dark grey suit . . . Burberry
raincoat . . . and a deerstalker hat. And he was carrying a
travelling bag with his initials on it. I showed your Sergeant
one like it yesterday.' She opened her eyes and gazed at
Scobie busily writing.

'That's a very comprehensive description, Mrs Richmond,' said Millson. 'Thank you. And I wonder if we could
borrow a photograph of your husband?'

'I think there's one in here.' She stood up and went to a
drawer in the Welsh dresser. Lifting out an album she
extracted a photograph and gave it to him.

'Thank you.' Millson passed the photograph to Scobie.

Outside in the road, Millson opened the door of his car.
'Did you get the impression she was being a deal more
helpful than last time, Norris?'

'Definitely. Strikes me she wouldn't mind seeing her husband banged up so's she'd be free. I don't think she cares
for him one little bit.'

Millson was looking through the gap between the houses.
'They can see the shipyard from their back garden. Must
be a constant reminder of what they missed. I imagine
Philip Richmond was pretty miffed at being cut out of his
father's will.'

'Big disappointment for his wife too,' Scobie pointed out.

Millson closed the car door again. 'Let's have a word
with the neighbours while we're here.'

There was no one at home in the first house they called
at. In the second house, the woman there had seen Melissa
Richmond drive away Wednesday evening and her husband leave in his own car soon after. She hadn't actually
seen either of them return, but she'd heard their cars and
seen the reflection of headlights—one at about eleven
o'clock, the other around midnight.

'What about the next morning?' Millson asked.

Oh yes, she said, she'd seen Mrs Richmond drive off in the car with her husband last Thursday morning at eight o'clock.

Melissa watched through the curtains as Millson and Scobie drove away. The nosey cow next door had probably told them about her and Tom. Not that the woman could say much. She and Tom had been very discreet. And clever too. Melissa smiled, remembering a summer long ago.

'What are those red stains on your dress, Melissa? Have you cut yourself?'

'No, Auntie, we've been picking strawberries, Tommy and me. I must've wiped my fingers on my dress.'

Aunt Harriet had never suspected the truth. Their teen-age game had started as a tease—pretending to be small children playing mothers and fathers. It had gone on too long . . . become intense . . . until, suddenly, it was out of control.

Afterwards, poor Tommy had been horrified. 'You're bleeding, Missy!'

Melissa had been thirteen, Tom Lowery seventeen.

CHAPTER 13

Millson held the Press conference in front of the Incident Room trailer. He told reporters the police were following a number of useful leads on the murder of Janet West and inquiries were proceeding. As part of these inquiries he was anxious to trace a Mr Philip Richmond who left Findlesham last Thursday morning and might be travelling in the North of England. Anyone with information as to his whereabouts was asked to phone the Incident Room or their local police station.

'Is he a suspect?' a reporter asked.

'I can't answer that until we've spoken to him,' Millson said.

'Do you expect to make an early arrest?' asked another reporter.

'I can't say at the moment. But I'm hopeful of bringing the case to an early conclusion,' Millson said.

The inference was obvious, Scobie thought mournfully, as copies of Philip Richmond's photograph were distributed. Nicola Richmond would seize on it immediately.

'Shouldn't we forewarn Miss Richmond, if we're going to put out an alert for her father?' he'd asked Millson earlier.

'I don't see any need to do that,' Millson said. 'But you can if you want to.'

He hadn't, though. He'd been unwilling to face her inevitable questions and see the pain in her eyes when she realized they suspected her father of murder.

That evening, as Leonard Pearson sat drinking in the bar of the Anchor, he was approached by Tom Lowery.

'I hear the police have been questioning you again, Len.'

'Yep.' Pearson seemed in confident mood as he took a gulp of beer.

'What did they want?'

'Wanted to know if I'd heard or seen anything of that library woman being done in. Reckoned I must've had a ringside seat.' He uttered a snorting laugh.

'So what did you tell them?' Lowery asked.

'Told 'em I was having a kip in the rest-room so I didn't hear or see a thing. That's what I told 'em,' he boasted. 'I knew'd they'd find me hairs on the bed an' I got in first, see?' He smirked and took a mouthful of drink.

'What else did they ask you?'

'Dunno 'bout ask. They snitched a coupla hairs from me head. Won't prove nothing.' Pearson put a finger to the side of his nose. 'I boxed clever, see? I told 'em I'd had a kip on the bed before, so it didn't matter me hairs being there.'

'That was smart, Lenny.'

'Yeh. Smarter'n you think.'

'Really?' Lowery looked interested. He pointed to Pearson's empty glass. 'Got time for another before you go on duty, Lenny?'

Pearson glanced at his watch. 'Yeh, why not? Why friggin' not?'

'Tell us more, then,' Lowery invited, when he returned with the drinks.

At nine o'clock that evening Leonard Pearson completed his tour of the shipyard and returned to the small office in the shed by the gate. As he set out on his second tour at eleven o'clock, he could hear the distant clink of glasses in the bar of the Black Dog. The yard itself was silent.

Starting at the tall building that ran the length of the tidal dock, he checked the double doors behind which a pick-up truck was garaged, and then the single door next to them. He was surprised to find this door unlocked, because he was sure he'd checked it on his earlier round.

He opened the door and stepped inside, switching on his torch. As he swept the darkness with a beam of light it suddenly illuminated a figure standing close to him. He saw eyes glaring from a balaclava mask—a hand holding a knife—and turned to run. Before he could reach the door an arm was thrown round his neck bringing him to a halt.

A voice in his ear hissed, 'Keep quiet or I'll cut your throat!'

'Don't hurt me,' Pearson whined. 'I'll do anything you want.'

'Kneel!'

He fell to his knees and dropped the torch.

'Put your hands behind you!'

He did as he was told. Each hand was tied swiftly and expertly to an ankle. A foot prodded him and he toppled over on to his back. As he lay helpless, with his wrists strapped to his ankles, sticking-plaster was stretched across his mouth.

The hooded figure picked up the torch with a gloved hand and went to the rear of the pick-up truck where a dustbin bag and a long piece of rubber tubing lay on the floor. The man stooped and pushed one end of the tubing over the vehicle's exhaust pipe then picked up the bag and led the other end to Pearson. Bending down, he pulled the dustbin bag loosely over Pearson's head and shoulders, inserted the end of the tubing and secured tube and bag in position with a length of cord around Pearson's chest.

He climbed into the truck's cab and started the engine. A wave of nauseating fumes belched into the plastic bag and Pearson strained frantically at his bonds as deadly carbon monoxide flowed into his lungs.

The man monitored the second hand of his watch and after two minutes he switched off the engine and jumped down from the cab. Bending over his victim, he untied the bag and tube and flashed the torch on his face. Pearson was unconscious, but breathing. He pulled the sticking plaster carefully from his mouth, then took a handkerchief and a bottle of surgical spirit from his pocket, soaked the handkerchief in spirit and wiped any traces of adhesive from Pearson's mouth. Untying Pearson's hands and feet, he massaged his wrists and ankles to restore circulation and eliminate the marks left by the cords.

The man dragged Pearson to the truck and lifted him into the driving seat. He wound down the window, fed in the rubber tube and wound the window up again to hold it in place, then started the engine and closed the door. He stood for a while watching Pearson's unconscious body slumped over the steering-wheel with exhaust fumes pumping into the cab.

Finally, the man gathered all the items on the floor into the refuse bag and departed through the door.

In the cab, Leonard Pearson's face was turning cherry-red as he inhaled more carbon monoxide.

The telephone rang next morning as Millson was finishing shaving. Dena answered.

'Coppernob wants you, dad,' she called out.

Millson wiped his face on a towel and descended the stairs.

'Detective-Sergeant Scobie to you, my girl,' he said sternly. She made a face and stuck out her tongue at him, laughing with her eyes.

He picked up the phone. 'Pearson's dead,' Scobie told him. 'Suicide. The morning shift found him in a pick-up truck with a pipe from the exhaust into the driver's cab. I've told them not to touch anything.'

'I'll be there in half an hour,' Millson said.

Passing Dena on his way upstairs he landed a slap on her bottom. 'That's for being cheeky.'

She gave a yelp of pain. 'Child-beater!'

*

A uniformed constable stood by the door keeping out curious shipyard workers. The scene inside was one Millson
had witnessed several times before: a pipe from the exhaust
through a wound-up window, the flushed cheeks of the
victim. It was a common and convenient way to commit
suicide.

'Who found him?' he asked Scobie.

'One of the workmen. The engine had stopped. Must
have either overheated or run out of petrol.'

'Any suicide note?'

'Not that I can see.'

'Is the police surgeon here?'

'He's outside.' Scobie stepped to the door and signalled.

A bald, moon-faced man with heavy-framed spectacles
entered. 'All the signs of a straightforward suicide, Chief
Inspector. Apart from certifying the man as dead, there's
not much more I can tell you without a post-mortem.'

'How long has he been dead?'

'Judging by the body temperature and muscle rigidity,
I'd say between five and ten hours.'

Millson nodded and turned to Scobie. 'Has his wife been
informed?'

'Yes. It seems she rang in when he didn't come home at
his usual time this morning and they told her then.'

'We'd better walk up and have a word with her.'

Millson kept the interview with the distressed widow
brief. She told him she couldn't think of any reason for her
husband to kill himself and he'd seemed normal, even
happy, when he left for his night shift.

'He'd been a bit down for the last week, but he was more
cheerful after he saw you yesterday,' she said tearfully.

Millson frowned. 'Any idea why?'

She shook her head.

A furious Nicola Richmond intercepted them as they
walked across the car park to the Incident Room.

'There was a report about my father on the breakfast news. How *dare* you accuse him of that woman's murder!'

Her eyes were gleaming like a wildcat's and she was almost spitting at him. Millson expected the hair at the back of her neck was standing on end.

He said calmly, 'I did not accuse him. I said we were anxious to speak to him.'

'Don't bandy words! A reporter asked if he was a suspect and you as good as said he was.'

'A suspect is one thing, Miss Richmond. Proving guilt is another.'

'You haven't the slightest evidence to connect him with that woman and just because he's—'

'If I didn't have evidence I wouldn't put out a public alert for him,' Millson said sharply.

She gave a little gasp and looked at Scobie. He avoided her eyes.

'Now, if you'll excuse us,' Millson said. He walked on.

Scobie turned to follow him. 'Norris . . .' She laid a restraining hand on his arm. 'Is it bad about my father?'

He said awkwardly, 'I can't discuss the case, Nicola.'

'I see.' She looked down at the ground. 'With Pearson's suicide I'm a night-duty man short. But I suppose you still won't do anything about protecting the yard?'

Scobie shook his head. 'I can recommend a very good replacement, though.'

She looked up. 'Really? Who?'

'An ex-policeman I know. He's looking for night work so he can spend time in his garden during the day. I'll give him a ring if you like.'

'Oh yes! Thank you.' Impulsively, she planted a kiss on his cheek. She had to stand on her toes to reach.

Enlivened, he hurried after Millson. Before he caught up with him a man's voice behind called, 'Sergeant!' He turned and found a DC on his heels.

Minutes later an exuberant Scobie burst into Millson's

office. 'Guess what? They found this in Pearson's pocket.' He handed him a black notebook. 'Janet West's engagement diary. It's packed with initials and times.'

Millson opened the diary and turned the pages. 'Thoughtful of him to leave this in his pocket,' he said drily.

'Like a suicide note, you mean?'

'And a confession.'

'This puts Nicola's father in the clear, doesn't it?' Scobie asked eagerly.

'Not necessarily.' Millson stopped at a page and studied it. 'The day she was killed she had four appointments during the day, including—' he glanced up at Scobie—'one with PR—Philip Richmond. In the evening she had an appointment with LP at nine o'clock and KG at nine-thirty . . . obviously Leonard Pearson and Kevin Goodman.'

'Those appointments span the time she was killed,' Scobie reminded him. 'And they both said they didn't know her.'

Millson nodded. He laid down the diary and lit a cigarette. 'Goodman belonged to the library. Pearson didn't. And Laura Stebbing was very definite that Janet wouldn't meet anyone who didn't belong to the library. So why did she have an appointment with Pearson? And why did he kill himself?'

'Maybe he's the exception and that's why she didn't tell Laura about him. Anyway, the fact he had her diary makes him the murderer, surely? And obviously he killed himself because he thought we were on to him.'

'I distrust the obvious. Check PNC criminal records and see if Pearson had any convictions.' Millson drew on his cigarette and blew out smoke. 'And ask the lab to do a DNA test on him.'

'She wouldn't have had sex with a man like Pearson, would she?'

'I agree it seems unlikely, but let's find out.'

'Right.' Scobie made for the door. 'What do we tell the Press about Pearson?'

'Only that it looks like suicide and we're awaiting the post-mortem. We don't mention the diary.'

Scobie nodded. 'And Goodman? Bring him in for questioning?

'Not yet. After they've analysed the diary and we know what other meetings he had with her.' Millson put out his cigarette. 'A few days ago I didn't have a single suspect. Now, all of a sudden, I have three.' A glint of humour came into his eyes. 'One's dead, one's done a runner and the other's a scoutmaster.'

CHAPTER 14

The check of criminal records revealed that ten years ago Leonard Pearson had convictions for robbery with violence and demanding money with menaces.

'Presumably Nicola didn't know,' Scobie said. 'Gives us a possible motive. Laura Stebbing said Janet carried a lot of money in her bag. Presumably he took the diary because he was named in it and then kept it to use for blackmail perhaps.'

'We need more than motive, Norris. We need hard evidence—like the weapon and the place where she was killed.'

The analysis of the diary entries was completed at midday, the team having linked all the initials except Pearson's to members of the library. The analysis showed an occasional appointment with Philip Richmond on a Wednesday afternoon and regular appointments on Wednesday evenings with Leonard Pearson and Kevin Goodman.

'More or less every Wednesday fortnight,' Scobie commented, handing the catalogue of dates to Millson.

'Corresponding with the scout meetings, no doubt.' Millson studied the analysis. 'Though I don't see why Pearson's appointments should correspond with them.' He glanced at his watch. 'Where does Goodman work?'

'He manages a sports shop in Colchester. Shall I bring him in?'

'No . . . wait.' Millson drummed the table with his fingers. 'You remember that girl guide's uniform they fished out of the river? Where's the forensic report on it?'

'Filed in the outer office, I expect.'

'Let's have a look at it.'

Scobie went out and returned with a typewritten sheet. Millson scanned it, quoting intermittently. '. . . little worn . . . almost new . . . blouse . . . skirt . . . Ah! Here's what I was looking for. Female hairs on the collar of the blouse.'

'Well, what did you expect?' Scobie asked with a grin. 'Male ones?'

'You're missing the point, Norris. Phone the lab and ask them to compare the hair with Janet West's. Shouldn't take them more than a few minutes with a microscope.'

The answer came in half an hour. The hairs on the uniform were Janet West's. Millson put his hands between his knees and rubbed them together. It was a habit of his when he scored a success, Scobie noticed, the equivalent of a fighter pilot's victory roll.

'Now you can pick up Goodman,' Millson said.

Kevin Goodman was agitated when Scobie brought him into Millson's room in the Incident Room trailer. 'This is very inconvenient, Chief Inspector. Friday afternoon is a busy time and I've had to leave a junior in charge.' His normally pink cheeks were a deep red. 'The Sergeant tells me you want to see me in connection with your murder inquiry. I can't imagine why.'

'When we spoke to you before,' Millson said, 'you told us you didn't know Janet West.'

'Yes, that's right. Only to speak to in the library.'

'Then perhaps you'll explain why your initials appear regularly in her appointment diary on Wednesday nights.'

'Why the devil should the initials be mine?' Goodman demanded. 'There must be other people with the same initials as me.'

'Let me ask you about something else then . . . a girl guide's uniform.' Millson noted a tightening of Goodman's facial muscles. 'Divers found it on the riverbed not far from your scouts' barge. A complete outfit, wrapped in a plastic bag. What do you know about that?'

'Nothing.' Goodman's tone was truculent. 'The guides don't meet on the barge.'

'Exactly,' Millson said. 'So how did the uniform get there?'

Goodman shrugged his shoulders. 'How should I know?'

Millson leaned forward across the table. 'The clothes had been worn by Janet West. Her hairs were in the beret and all over the collar of the blouse.'

Goodman remained silent, staring ahead and stiff-faced.

'We know about Janet's activities and her library clients,' Millson continued. 'And it's my belief that you were one. If we search that hut on the barge, do you suppose we won't find evidence she's been there? More hairs, for example?'

Goodman maintained his silence for a moment longer. Then he said, 'Oh God,' and sagged in his chair.

Millson waited. The man looked about to fall apart, ready to pour out a confession. Juries were wary of confessions these days. They'd been the basis of too many wrong convictions. Millson wished they were at Colchester police station where he could have recorded the interview.

Kevin Goodman sat up, his eyes moving from Millson to Scobie and back again. 'All right. I did know her. I met her through the library and we started talking. She was very understanding . . . kind . . . warm . . .' Goodman's eyes met Millson's, slewed away again. 'It's not a crime,' he muttered.

'What isn't?' Millson demanded.

'To look at a woman . . . have her dress up for you . . . enjoy fantasizing. There's no law against it.'

'Is that what she did for you?' Millson asked. 'Dressed up as a girl guide? That turned you on, did it?' When Goodman didn't answer he went on, 'And then you had sex?'

Goodman's head jerked up. 'No! It wasn't like that.' He

said desperately, 'Look, I don't have to go into details or explain what—'

'You admit you had an appointment with her at nine-thirty on the night she was killed?'

'Yes. But she didn't turn up.'

'I see.' Millson drew a deep breath and let it out in a long sigh.

'She didn't, I tell you! I was expecting her but she didn't come!'

Millson asked impassively, 'So what did you do?'

'I waited for a while and then I went home.'

Scobie turned the pages of his notebook. 'When we interviewed you before you said you arrived home a few minutes after nine. You couldn't have done, could you? Not if you expected Janet at nine-thirty and waited a while after that.'

'No, it was about ten when I got home.'

'It must have been later than that,' Scobie said. 'It would take at least a quarter of an hour to walk along the river-bank, through the shipyard and then up Anglesea Road to your house.'

'I didn't go that way,' Goodman said quickly. 'I told you before . . . I took a short cut across the fields.'

'Oh yes, some TV programme you wanted to watch, I believe,' Millson said sarcastically.

'Well, actually it was to get home before my wife. Her WI meeting finished at half ten.'

'I see. Let me recap on what you've told us, Mr Goodman,' said Millson. 'You were expecting Janet West at the scout hut at nine-thirty to dress up for you as a girl guide. She didn't arrive. You waited for a time and then you went home across the fields, arriving there at ten o'clock. Is that right?'

Goodman nodded. 'Yes, that's correct.'

'Then how did the uniform she was bringing come to be in the river?'

'She didn't bring it with her. We had regular appointments and kept it in the hut to save her traipsing it back and forth. I saw no reason to keep it after her death, so I threw it in the river.'

'In other words you destroyed evidence,' Millson said. 'That's a serious matter.'

'Evidence of what? I've done nothing wrong.' Goodman's voice had gained strength. 'What I did is not a crime,' he said firmly.

Millson cut him down. 'Murder is,' he said.

'*I didn't kill her!*'

Millson said relentlessly, 'You had an appointment with her on the barge at nine-thirty . . . the pathologist puts time of death at around that time . . . her body was found less than a hundred yards away . . . and you admit throwing her uniform in the river. Now, what happened? Did you quarrel? Did she threaten to tell your wife about your little games?'

'No!' Goodman shouted. 'I've told you! I didn't see her that night.'

Listening to Millson winding Goodman up, Scobie was relieved the interview wasn't being taped. A court might regard this as hostile questioning.

Abruptly, Millson changed direction. 'That wheelbarrow on the barge. Tell me again what it's used for.'

'Taking rubbish to the village tip.'

'The man who killed Janet West used a wheelbarrow. He carted her body along the riverbank in it and dumped her like a load of rubbish.'

Goodman said desperately, 'I've told you. Janet didn't come to the barge that evening.'

'Did you lie in wait for her then?' Millson asked. 'Somewhere along the path in the dark?'

'NO!' Goodman's hysterical shout in the confined space made Scobie jump. 'You're twisting everything. I want to see a solicitor.'

Millson said calmy, 'You're not under arrest, Mr Goodman. You can leave whenever you want. But my officers will now carry out a thorough search of the barge and I'd like you to go with them.'

Goodman hesitated. 'I'm not sure about another search.'

'I can detain you here while I apply for a magistrate's warrant,' Millson said coldly.

'No, all right,' Goodman said sullenly.

In the afternoon Millson reviewed the responses received so far to his appeal for information about Philip Richmond. There was the usual rash of doubtful and unlikely sightings and three positive ones from passengers on the train to London. A DC had already confirmed with the ticket-collector at Colchester station that a man carrying a travel bag with the initials PR on it and answering Richmond's description had boarded the London-bound train that Thursday morning, so he was no further forward.

In the late afternoon the detectives who'd searched the scout barge reported they'd found no signs of blood and no murder weapon. Hair samples had been taken from the sofa and other places and been sent to the forensic laboratory. Millson had no doubt that some of them would be Janet West's. As with those in the rest-room, that only established she had been there at some time, not that she was there on the night she was murdered.

'I'm off home,' Millson told Scobie. 'There's nothing doing here and Dena's cooking the dinner tonight.'

It was his reward. 'I saw you on telly yesterday,' Dena had said ominously. 'Your suit was creased, your shirt was undone and you looked a mess.'

'How I look is my business,' he said, resenting the criticism.

'You might think of me,' she said. 'I get a lot of stick from the kids at school. They all know you're my dad.'

It was a point Millson hadn't considered. 'All right, young lady, you've made your point.'

'You should ditch that old suit,' Dena said. 'You've got better ones. And wear a decent tie.'

'Will do,' he'd promised.

Scobie said, 'That's nice. Something exotic, will it be?'

'No. Egg and bacon is her limit.' Millson smiled happily. 'Fortunately, I like it. Never have time in the morning.'

As Millson's car drove away a WPC approached Scobie. 'There was a message from Miss Richmond, Sergeant. She says she's delighted with the man you recommended and will you please join her for a thank-you drink in the Black Dog at six o'clock.' The WPC gave him a conspiratorial wink. 'I didn't think I'd better pass that on while you were with the Chief Inspector.'

Scobie knew he shouldn't accept Nicola's invitation. She was the daughter of a suspect and if Philip Richmond came to trial, Scobie's socializing with his daughter could prejudice the prosecution's case. Yet she would think him churlish if he refused. She only wanted to thank him. And for what? For obtaining employment for a retired policeman. Nothing compromising in that.

She was already there when he entered the bar. At this hour the bar was almost empty, but even if it had been packed he could hardly have failed to see her. She was wearing a royal blue *cheongsam*. It was brightly patterned and split to the waist. Long pendant ear-rings dangled from her ears and she was holding a gold evening bag. With her short, slim, figure and raven hair, she could have passed for Chinese.

She smiled with amusement as he approached her with open-mouthed appraisal. 'I'm going out to dinner and then to the theatre,' she explained.

So he needn't have worried. She wasn't planning to ply him with drink and pump him about the case.

'You've engaged Mike Kitchin already, then?' he said cheerfully. 'That was quick.'

'I'm a fast worker, didn't you know?' She laughed up at him. 'What'll you have?'

She ordered the drinks and when they were served she raised her glass. 'I'm very grateful. Thank you.'

'It was nothing,' he said.

'Oh, but it was. I shall feel the yard is in safe hands when he's on duty.' The dark blue eyes regarded him over the rim of the glass. 'Do you have a girlfriend, Norris?'

He hesitated. 'Yes and no.'

'And what does that mean?'

He explained the situation between him and Kathy.

'How very odd,' she said. 'What's the matter with the girl? Can't she make up her mind?'

Scobie felt a pang of disloyalty as he said he thought that was exactly what the trouble was. 'And you? Boyfriend?' he asked.

'Too busy. No time,' she said briskly.

'You'll make time one day, I expect.'

'Oh yes. When I meet the right man.' She gave him a roguish look. 'I'm impossible to live with, you know. Utterly spoilt and used to having my own way.'

'Comes of having all those men taking orders from you, I expect,' he said jokingly.

She smiled. 'When my grandfather died I called them together and told them if they thought I was a soft touch, to think again. "I'm Bertram Richmond's granddaughter," I said, "and I'm as hard as he was. But my teeth are sharper and so's my bite."' She laughed. 'I never had any trouble after that.'

No, I'll bet you didn't, he thought, you're a right little martinet. Adorable, though.

'There was another reason I wanted to talk to you, Norris,' she said, putting down her drink.

Oh-oh, here it comes after all, he warned himself. She's

going to ask what evidence we have against her father.

She saw his change of expression. 'No, I'm *not* going to ask you about my father,' she said.

She always said 'my father', he noticed, never 'Dad' or 'Daddy'. He wondered about their relationship.

'The launching is set for high tide on Wednesday,' she went on, 'and provided there are no more dirty tricks, we'll make it. I wondered if you could pay Andrew Hartman a visit. If he knew the police were taking an interest, he wouldn't dare try anything. Couldn't you say I've reported the sabotage and you're making inquiries? That would be enough to put him off. You don't have to accuse him of anything.'

'You still think he's behind it?'

'I can't see who else.'

'I suppose I could do that,' Scobie said cautiously. It would have to be sometime tomorrow when Mr Millson wasn't around. 'Does Hartman work Saturdays?'

'Yes. The man's a workaholic. Seven days a week.'

'Right. I'll see what I can do.'

'Thanks.' She glanced at her watch. 'I must go.' She downed her drink.

He accompanied her outside to her car. She turned and leaned back against the car door. 'That was nice, Norris. And thank you again.' She stood with her face tilted up, baby-like mouth slightly open.

Afterwards he cursed himself. She'd expected him to kiss her and he'd hesitated. Only for an instant, while he suppressed his disloyalty to Kathy. The delay had been fatal. She turned away and opened the door.

''Bye, then.' She slipped into the driving seat and closed the door.

His disappointment lasted all the way home to his flat in Colchester and on into the rest of the evening. He vowed not to waste another chance like that.

CHAPTER 15

The result of the DNA test on Philip Richmond's hair came through on Saturday morning. He was not the man who'd been intimate with Janet West on the night of her death.

Scobie phoned the information to Millson at his home. Millson had taken the morning off to attend his daughter's hockey match at school. Scobie hoped he would revise his opinion of Richmond as a suspect.

But Millson said, 'OK, so he wasn't her lover. Doesn't mean he isn't her killer. He knew her . . . he was out of his house at the time of the murder . . . he left unexpectedly the next morning . . . and despite a national appeal, he hasn't contacted us. Until those matters are cleared up he remains a suspect.'

Andrew Hartman's offices in Ipswich were in a prestige location overlooking the former docks where an old warehouse had been turned into offices. His own room on the top floor, with a fine view over the Orwell, was enormous.

Like Nicola Richmond before him, Scobie was struck by Andrew Hartman's compelling authority and charismatic charm. He suspected that if you were in the way of this powerfully-built man with the steel-grey hair, he would smile pleasantly as he steamrollered you into the ground.

Scobie's prepared approach was made redundant by Hartman's reaction to the cause of his visit.

'Sabotage? She accused *me* of being responsible for that last time I phoned her,' Hartman said, leaning forward from his executive armchair and eyeing Scobie critically. 'You haven't come here peddling the same accusation, have you, Sergeant?'

Scobie was suddenly uneasy. This was not a man you

accused without irrefutable evidence and he didn't have any. 'There's no accusation, Mr Hartman,' he said swiftly. 'Miss Richmond has asked for police protection and I'm merely seeking information.'

'Well then, let me tell you that dirty tricks are not my style,' Hartman said. 'I've made the girl a very generous offer—anyone who understands land values will confirm that for you. The shipyard's finished. My people have researched it thoroughly. There isn't another order in sight after the present vessel is launched and you can't keep a shipyard going without orders. She'll have to accept my offer in the end. She's just being stubborn.'

Scobie asked cautiously, 'Is it possible someone on your staff is trying to hurry things up without your knowledge?'

Hartman sat back in his chair, a finger across his lips, considering the question. 'Nope,' he said after a moment, 'that one won't run. Perhaps someone has a grudge against her.'

'Do you know of anyone?'

Hartman puffed out his cheeks. 'The environmentalists maybe.'

'I don't follow.'

'Greenpeace . . . Friends of the Earth . . . or some more extreme group.'

'I still don't follow,' Scobie said.

Hartman sighed. 'The *Vivacity* is being built to carry toxic waste.'

'Oh,' said Scobie, taken aback. 'She didn't tell me that.'

'I don't think the little lady knows, old son. The company who commissioned the ship have kept very quiet about it.'

'How did you find out?'

Hartman looked pained. 'Sergeant, my research boys winkle out *everything*. That's what they're paid to do. They've even given me a psychological profile on Miss Richmond. "Obstinate, will struggle to the very end," they say.' He smiled sadly. 'I confess I'm sorry for her. She's such a pretty little thing.'

'You've met her?'

'I took her to lunch once. Tried to interest her in the development plan. She sent me away with a flea in the ear.' The recollection brought a rueful expression to his face. 'No one has done that to me before.'

'You could hardly expect her to be interested in a scheme that would close the shipyard. It was left to her by her grandfather and it's been in existence since Tudor times,' Scobie told him.

'History!' Hartman retorted. 'When a business is finished, it's finished. You have to make way for something new.'

'Like a housing estate,' Scobie said scathingly.

Hartman's face darkened with annoyance. 'You don't know what you're talking about, Sergeant. Here, let me show you.'

He stood up from his desk, dwarfing Scobie, who rose with him, by several inches and crossed the room to a scale model laid out on a platform under the window. He pressed some buttons and began pointing out the features: ' . . .landscaped gardens . . . a small park . . . tennis courts . . .'

Scobie gazed at the illuminated model in awe. Where Janet West's body had lain was a floodlit riverside promenade. And the wet dock in the shipyard had been enlarged and converted into a marina. The entire area had been transformed with imagination and taste.

'Is this the housing estate you're scoffing at?' Hartman demanded.

'No, it's magnificent,' Scobie was forced to admit. 'I like the idea of a marina. Tanniford needs one.' Somewhere to keep his boat, he thought, if he and Kathy came together again.

'Perhaps you could persuade Nicola Richmond of its merits?' Hartman suggested hopefully.

Scobie shook his head. No matter how worthy and enlightened the development plan, it could never appeal to Nicola because its implementation spelt the end of the yard. The shipyard was doomed. He could see that now and it depressed him. It would break her heart.

He glanced at the 48 inch to the mile Ordnance Survey plan on the wall above the model. It showed the present disposition of the land and each plot was marked and numbered. His attention was caught by an unexpected boundary line. He stepped closer, peering at it. He turned to Hartman.

'Won't you have to provide an access road for vehicles if you want planning permission for this project?'

'Of course.'

'Well, according to this Ordnance Survey map, the access to the shipyard is only single track along the edge of a piece of waste ground the workers use as a car park. The rest of the waste ground is a separate plot. It doesn't belong to the shipyard.'

Hartman's eyes crinkled in a smile. 'Very observant of you, Sergeant. I see why you're a detective.'

Scobie pursued the point. 'The shipyard land is no use to you without that plot. The track is only twelve feet wide.'

'Absolutely right. But you don't imagine I've gone this far without securing that extra piece of land, do you? I took an option to buy it six months ago. It's going to cost a bomb, but the owners had me over a barrel.'

'Who owns it?'

Hartman's eyebrows came together in a frown. 'Does this have any connection with your murder inquiry?'

'It might. I imagine the owner of that plot stands to make a lot of money if you buy the shipyard and take up your option?'

Hartman nodded. 'Five hundred thousand pounds, to be precise.'

Scobie's interest quickened. 'But nothing if you don't?'

'Only the option money—twenty thousand.'

'So, whoever owns that plot has a considerable interest in your scheme going ahead?'

'Yep, you can say that.'

'And a bit of sabotage to delay the launching of the ship and bankrupt Miss Richmond would make sure of it, no doubt?'

Hartman pursed his lips. 'Yep, I'm following your drift, Sergeant.'

'Which raises the possibility the murdered woman encountered a man about to do some damage to the shipyard and he killed her to avoid identification.'

Hartman smiled with admiration. 'A nice piece of deduction. You've convinced me of a connection, my friend.'

'It's worth investigating, anyway,' Scobie said modestly. 'So, who owns the plot?'

'As I recall, it was the executors of someone's estate. I don't believe we know the actual owner. The option was dealt with through solicitors, of course. They may be able to help you.'

Hartman stretched out a hand and pressed a buzzer on his desk. A girl appeared at his door instantly, like a genie. He gave an order and the girl withdrew. Seconds later she reappeared with a folder, glided forward and handed it to him. Scobie half-expected her to curtsey as she glided away again.

Hartman opened the folder and leafed through the enclosures. 'Poulson Bannerman in Colchester were the solicitors,' he told Scobie.

It was a forlorn hope that a solicitor's would be open on a Saturday, but Scobie called there on his way back and when it wasn't he drove on to Tanniford.

There was another possible source of information—and this one was open on a Saturday. He swallowed his pride, and called in at Kathy Benson's estate agency in the High Street.

'It's an official visit, Kathy,' he said as she looked up from her desk with a smile.

'Oh.' The smile died.

'That piece of waste ground in front of the shipyard . . . do you know who it belongs to?

'I thought it belonged to the shipyard.'

'No, only the cinder track across it from the road to the entrance. The rest is a separate plot.'

'I can look through our old records, if you like. They go back about fifty years. If we handled a sale or purchase it'll be recorded.'

'Thanks, Kathy. If you would, please.'

He followed her into a rear room lined with filing cabinets. After searching through several drawers, she shook her head. 'Sorry. Nothing. Is it important?'

'It might be very important.'

'OK, I'll ask my dad. He might know.' Kathy's father had run the estate agency before he retired and handed it over to Kathy.

She lifted the phone and keyed a number. After a minute or two of conversation she hung up.

'He remembers there being a derelict building on the site when he was a boy. He says you can still see the remains of the foundations. He's no idea who owned it, but he's going to ask Grandad. He'll know if anyone does.'

Kathy's grandfather was ninety-four and lived in an old people's home. Scobie would have to wait for his information until tomorrow, Sunday, Kathy told him, when her father would be visiting Grandad as usual.

The post-mortem report on Leonard Pearson arrived in the afternoon, soon after Millson returned from watching his daughter play hockey. There were no signs of violence or suspicious marks on the body and death was due to carbon monoxide poisoning.

The result of the DNA profiling was phoned from Aldermaston an hour later. It proved that Pearson had had sex with Janet West shortly before she died.

'That's that, then,' Scobie said, then caught the glint in Millson's eyes. 'Well, isn't it? Suicide . . . possession of the diary . . . previous convictions . . . And now this, proving he was with her that night. Motive, opportunity, presence at the scene . . . what more do we want?'

'We don't have the weapon and we don't know where she was killed. The man's dead, Norris! Which means we have to be doubly careful.'

'How d'you mean?'

'He can't speak for himself, we can't question him and it's all too easy to hang a crime on a dead man because he can't answer back. Let me ask you this. If he were alive, would you charge him with murder solely on that evidence?'

'No, but I'd arrest him on suspicion and question him.'

'That's exactly the point. You can't arrest a dead man and you can't question him to arrive at the truth. So let's not be hasty. After all—' Millson grinned sardonically— 'he can't run away.'

WDC Bennett had interviewed nine scouts. Her map was criss-crossed with lines from the scout barge to various addresses in Tanniford and one outside the village at Tanniford Cross. None of the boys had seen anything of help to the murder investigation. Two of the scouts on her list were unavailable. One was with his parents in Canada visiting relatives. The other was on holiday in Cyprus.

That left only the twelfth boy, Jimmy Monk.

CHAPTER 16

Scobie had been expecting a phone call or a visit from Kathy Benson to convey whatever information her father had gleaned from her grandfather. Instead, on Monday morning a typewritten report was delivered to the Incident Room by her clerk, Gerald Turner. There was no covering note and the report was impersonal. It didn't begin, *Darling Norrie*, or even *Dear Norris*, but was headed: '*Detective-Sergeant Scobie. For information*'. He shrugged. Well, if that's the way she felt . . .

He read the report. Grandad Benson, it seemed, was a living encylopædia. Tanniford had been much smaller when he was a child at the turn of the century and there had been a cart track round the outside of the village to transport supplies and materials from the station to the shipyard. Later, the railway company extended a branch line to Brightlingsea, then a thriving fishing port, to convey fish direct to Billingsgate. The line severed the cart track to the shipyard and from then on goods arriving at Tanniford station had to be delivered to the yard via East Street.

In those days there had been a field in front of the shipyard. It belonged to the Bridewell family who lived in Tendring. The field was fenced off from the cinder track alongside it that led to the shipyard entrance and in the First World War the field had been turned into a smallholding where the family kept pigs. It was abandoned after the war. The pigstys became derelict and over the years the fencing, pigstys and boundaries gradually disappeared. By the nineteen-sixties, when more and more workers were driving to work by car, the waste ground in front of the shipyard was being used as a car park and everyone believed it belonged to the yard.

William Bridewell, who owned the original field, had died in nineteen-seventy and his estate had passed to his unmarried daughter, Harriet. She had since died—Kathy's grandfather had seen a report of her death in the papers some time last year—and he believed the estate had now passed to a brother.

Scobie phoned Kathy to thank her and her grandfather for their help. 'That's all right.' Her voice was cold.

He said provocatively, 'I thought we agreed to be polite to each other.'

'I am being polite, damn you!' She slammed down the phone.

'What have I done now?' Scobie muttered at the handset.

At her end of the line Kathy hesitated over whether to call him back and apologize. Her pride wouldn't let her, though, and anyway it was his own fault, she thought. Yesterday evening she'd met her father in the Black Dog to take notes of his visit to Grandfather. When they ordered their drinks Ted, the barman, told her Norris was in the bar Saturday night with Nicola Richmond, the shipyard heiress.

'All dolled-up,' she was,' Ted said. 'You could see she was on the prowl. They had a drink and left together.'

Kathy tried to be objective. Norris was a free agent. She herself had made him one. If he chose to swan off with Nicola Richmond . . . The pencil she was holding tightly between her fingers suddenly broke. She glared at the two halves in her hands. Now look what he'd made her do!

In the middle of the morning Mrs Pearson walked in to the Incident Room and asked to speak to the officer in charge. Her white hair was uncombed and her cheeks were puffy with crying.

'You've got to stop it!' she said when she was ushered in to Millson. 'They're saying terrible things in the village about my Lennie. It ain't right. It ain't right at all. And him only dead three days.'

Millson put on a sympathetic face. 'What are they saying, Mrs Pearson?'

'They're saying Lennie was meeting the Book Lady on the sly and he killed himself 'cos the police were going to arrest him for murdering her. He didn't even *know* her.' The moist eyes appealed to him anxiously. 'Did he, Mr Millson?'

Scobie glanced at Millson wondering if he would tell her.

'We're still investigating these matters, Mrs Pearson,' Millson said smoothly. 'In the meantime, I can assure you these rumours have not come from the police.'

'Then it must be Tom Lowery that's putting them around. And him supposed to be Lennie's friend.' She sniffed. 'He's no better than he should be. Him and that Mrs Richmond.'

Scobie said, 'I thought he did the gardening.'

'Gardening? Huh! First time I've heard it called that. Lennie told me about them. Tom sneaks up there from his houseboat when her husband's away and—' Eleanor Pearson checked herself. Anyway,' she went on, 'he shouldn't put lies around about my husband. Lennie mayn't have been snow white, but he was no killer.'

She turned to Millson. 'Is it right she was put in a wheelbarrow? That's the rumour in the village.'

He was about to tell her he couldn't discuss the case when he was riveted by her next statement.

'Lennie couldn't do that, you see. He couldn't use his right arm.'

Millson stared at her, taking it in. 'Are you saying your husband was disabled, Mrs Pearson?'

'Oh, he wouldn't have liked to be called that,' she said earnestly. 'Len was sensitive and didn't let on about his difficulty. It didn't really notice, you see.'

'Was this a temporary affliction?'

'Oh no. He's been like it for years. "Frozen shoulder", they call it.'

'Would you mind waiting outside for a moment?' Millson said. 'Norris, have someone organize a cup of tea for Mrs Pearson.'

Scobie took her arm and led her out. When he returned Millson was on the phone to the pathologist.

'Did the post-mortem on Leonard Pearson reveal any infirmity or disability?'

'I'll have to refer to my notes. Hang on a moment.' There was a crackling of paper at the other end of the line. 'Yes. He had severe osteo-arthritis in the right shoulder. The joint was markedly deformed. Nothing to do with the cause of death, of course.'

'Would he have been capable of delivering those blows to Janet West's head?'

'Hardly. I'd be surprised if he was able to raise his arm above shoulder level.'

'What about lifting her body into a barrow and wheeling it a hundred yards or so?'

'Absolutely not.'

Millson clicked his tongue. 'I suppose there's no doubt his death *was* suicide?'

'Why, what do you have in mind?'

'That he might have been tied up when he was put in the vehicle and untied after he was dead.'

'There would have been marks on the wrists and ankles. Any restriction of circulation at the time of death would show up as œdema. And there wasn't any.'

'Thank you, doctor.' Millson put down the phone. 'Pearson couldn't have killed Janet West,' he told Scobie. 'He hadn't the strength. Nor could he have wheeled her body about in a wheelbarrow.'

Millson went to the door and looked out. Eleanor Pearson was sitting beside the door, sipping tea. He lowered himself into a chair next to her.

'You can tell everyone you've spoken to me, Mrs Pearson, and I've told you we're satisfied your husband had no connection with the murder of Janet West.'

Her face lit up. 'Can I? Can I say that? Oh, I'm so relieved. I couldn't have faced the funeral with that suspicion hanging over him.' She put down her cup and stood up. 'I wish I knew why he killed himself, though. Do you know, Mr Millson?'

He said gently, 'No, I don't, Mrs Pearson. I'm afraid you may never know.'

He returned to his room. 'Well, that's one suspect less,' he said.

'I think we may have a new one,' said Scobie, taking the opportunity to mention his visit to Andrew Hartman.

He let Millson think the visit arose from Kathy's grandfather telling him about the plot of land, not that it was in response to Nicola's request to scare Hartman.

'The person who owns the plot will receive half a million from Hartman if the deal goes through,' Scobie explained. 'That's a powerful reason for a campaign of sabotage to make Miss Richmond sell.'

'I agree, Norris, but where's this leading?' Millson asked.

'It leads us back to the possibility that Janet West ran into someone committing damage and he killed her to avoid detection. You didn't think much of the idea before. But it's worth following up, isn't it?'

Millson thought about it for a while. 'All right. Find out who owns the land and see what that gives us.'

A voice on the phone at Poulson Bannerman's informed Scobie that under the terms of her will, which his firm had had the pleasure of executing, Harriet Bridewell had bequeathed her cottage and a plot of land in Tanniford to her brother, John Bridewell. He being deceased, these passed to his only child, Irene Bridewell.

'So this Irene Bridewell now owns the plot?'

'That is correct and upon her instructions we negotiated the option to purchase with Mr Hartman's company solicitors.'

'May I have her address?'

'She lives at the aunt's cottage in Tendring. It's called St Crispin's.'

Millson opened a folder on his desk and went through the responses to last Thursday's appeal for information on the whereabouts of Philip Richmond.

Half a dozen people reported seeing a man answering Philip Richmond's description and carrying the distinctive black travel bag bearing his initials. Browsing through the reports Millson was struck by the fact that all the sightings had occurred either on the platform at Colchester or very early on in the train journey. No one had come forward who had seen him later in the journey, or at Liverpool Street, or anywhere else for that matter.

He read one of the statements again. It had been taken over the phone from a man who said he'd seen Richmond entering the toilet soon after the train left Colchester. Apparently they had both been heading for the same toilet, but Richmond got there first. The witness had waited for a while, then walked through a carriage to the next toilet. By the time he returned, Richmond had left the other toilet, because he saw another man emerge from it and stand by the carriage door as the train slowed down for its stop at Witham.

Millson lounged back in his chair, hands behind his head, thinking.

There was a telephone number after the address at the top of the statement. A note in brackets said the witness, Greg Bailey, worked from home.

Millson picked up the phone and rang him. He took him briefly through the statement to remind him of it and then asked him to describe Philip Richmond again.

'Clean-shaven, medium height and dark, greying hair. He had glasses and he wore a small-brimmed hat and a fawn Burberry raincoat. And he was carrying a black "Antler" travel bag with the initials PR.'

'You're remarkably observant, Mr Bailey.'

'It's a habit. I'm a systems analyst.'

'Uh-huh. Then tell me about the second man,' Millson invited. 'The one you saw coming out of the same loo as you returned to your seat.'

'He was walking ahead of me so I didn't really see his face, but I'm sure he was clean-shaven. Dark-haired . . . medium height . . . no glasses. Blue baseball cap on his head . . . wearing a dark anorak.'

'Young? Old?'

'Middling, I'd say.'

'Anything else you noticed?'

'Yes, he was carrying a haversack.'

'Ah . . .' Millson said with interest. 'What like?'

'It was fairly big and it looked full. Royal blue.'

'Thank you. You've been very helpful, Mr Bailey.'

Millson hung up and lit a cigarette. Could Philip Richmond have been carrying a change of clothes and a folded haversack in his travel bag? It would have been simple enough to swap clothes in the toilet, remove his glasses and put everything into the haversack, including the Antler bag. Then perhaps darken his grey hairs with blacking and come out of the toilet as a different man. That would explain why there were no sightings of him later than Witham. And if he *had* changed his clothes and darkened his hair the description issued to the media was now useless.

Why do it so soon after leaving Colchester, though? Why not wait until he reached Liverpool Street? Perhaps he hadn't gone to Liverpool Street. Millson recalled a passage in the report of the DC who'd questioned the ticket-collector at Colchester station. Apparently Richmond had made a point of asking if the train went to Liverpool Street. That was why the ticket-collector remembered him and his distinctive bag. Had Richmond deliberately drawn attention to himself? To lay a false trail?

Millson mulled over the problem for two more cigarettes, then opened his door and barked at a clerk, 'I want a DC to go to Witham station.'

St Crispin's had an unlived-in appearance, even from the road, when Scobie pulled up on the grass verge outside. No one answered the door to his knock and when he pushed open the flap of the letter-box, he saw a heap of advertising circulars on the mat. He walked round to the rear and peered through the kitchen window. The kitchen was tidy and bare, showing no signs of use. Returning to his car, he called Poulson Bannerman's on his mobile phone.

'Well, that's where we write to,' he was told, 'and receive answers from.'

Scobie left the car and walked along the lane to the next property. A middle-aged woman answered the door. Yes, she had known Harriet Bridewell. Not very well, though.

'We only moved here two years ago,' she explained.

Did she know who lived there now? Well, no one did. A woman called occasionally to pick up letters—the old lady's niece, she believed, though she hadn't spoken to her. She assumed the cottage was to be sold eventually, when the recession in the property market was over.

Scobie returned to the cottage. There was a Yale nightlatch on the front door. He took a credit card from his wallet, inserted it between door and frame, then forced it round the edge of the door and pushed it between lock and keeper. He flexed the card and the door sprang open. Stepping inside, he closed the door behind him.

He wandered through the rooms looking for clues to the whereabouts of Irene Bridewell. A family photograph stood on the sideboard in the front room. There seemed something vaguely familiar about one of the little girls in it.

He picked it up. Her eyes held him ... knowing eyes, half-covered by unusually heavy lids which gave a sly expression to the face. He turned the photo over. Written on the back was: *To Auntie Harriet from John, Clara and Missy.*

Missy ... A bell rang in Scobie's memory. Lowery had called Melissa Richmond 'Missy'. He'd taken it as a workman's colloquialism like 'Missus' for Miss or Mrs. Now, as he looked again at the photograph, he realized who the child's face reminded him of. Had 'Missy' been a pet name for Melissa?

He returned to his car and phoned Nicola Richmond. 'What was your stepmother's maiden name?'

'Bridewell.' He felt a surge of excitement. 'Did she have any sisters, do you know?'

'I don't think so. Why are you so interested in Melissa?'

'I'm not, unless I can link her to an Irene Bridewell.'

Nicola laughed. 'She *is* Irene Bridewell ... Irene Melissa Bridewell. She hates the name Irene. She's always used her middle name.'

CHAPTER 17

Irene Melissa Bridewell hated the name Irene from the time she watched *The Forsyte Saga* on television as a child. She switched to her second name at the age of thirteen when she met Tom Lowery.

Each summer she spent a fortnight of her school holiday with her Aunt Harriet at her cottage in Tendring. One year her aunt decided to have an overgrown area at the bottom of her long garden cleared and dug over for vegetables. She engaged Tom Lowery, the son of the cowman at a nearby farm, to do the job. He started on it the day Melissa arrived.

She wandered down the garden soon after he'd begun work. 'What's your name, boy?' she asked.

'Me name's Tom, an' doan you call me "Boy".'

She watched him plunge the spade into the ground, put his foot on it, lever up a sod of earth, then turn it over and raise the spade again to repeat the process.

'Whass yourn?' he asked, without breaking the rhythm of his digging.

'I'm—' She stopped. She would not be called Irene any longer. 'My name's Melissa,' she said.

He paused, rested his rough hands on the handle of the spade and looked at her. She stood boldly, golden hair shining in the sun, as his light blue eyes roamed over her.

He gave her a slow smile. 'I's'll call you "Missy",' he said.

It was Melissa and not her aunt who brought him a Thermos of tea mid-morning and mid-afternoon. Each time she dallied for a while, talking to him. The dark-haired country lad was very different from the boys in her co-ed school in Kensington. His coarse speech, rough manners and the steady rhythm of his body glistening with sweat as he worked stripped to the waist aroused disturbing sensations in the pubescent Melissa.

On the day it rained, she found him sheltering in the summer-house when she ran down the garden with the Thermos of tea. As she handed it to him the rain suddenly grew heavier, bucketing down the roof of the summer-house.

'You'm trapped here,' he said, uncapping the Thermos with calloused hands.

'That's right, I'm your prisoner,' she teased. 'What are you going to do with me?'

He looked down at his boots. Tom Lowery knew a lot about the land and how to deal with farm animals. He knew nothing of smart young city girls like Melissa. 'I doan know,' he said.

She was disappointed by his lack of initiative. 'Do you want to play mothers and fathers to pass the time?' she asked mockingly.

'Thass a kid's game,' he said scornfully.

'Not the way I play it,' she said.

The rain had long ceased when they eventually emerged from the summer-house.

From then on, when Melissa brought his tea each morning and afternoon, they went into the summer-house and she kept watch through the latticed window in case her aunt came down the garden to see what they were up to.

At the end of her holiday they made fervent promises to write to each other. Neither kept them, but Melissa never forgot the intense excitement of those times in the summer-house or the hard-muscled farm boy she'd shared them with.

After she left school she went to work in a firm of City accountants. When Philip Richmond joined the staff some years later and Melissa discovered he was heir to a shipyard, she set out to net him. It wasn't difficult. She was young and attractive and forty-five-year-old Philip, who'd been living with his father since his wife died ten years earlier, yearned to be married and have a home of his own again.

Melissa was not troubled by her father-in-law's hostility to the marriage, expecting it to fade in time. But when Bertram Richmond died two years later and left his entire estate, including the shipyard, to his granddaughter, Melissa's world collapsed. All her plans had been made on the assumption Philip would inherit the shipyard.

She felt cheated. She was twenty-seven and married to a man twenty years older than herself whom she didn't love. While marriage without love was a price she'd been prepared to pay for being the wife of a shipyard magnate like Bertram Richmond, she did not intend to remain married to a middle-aged man with no prospects.

However, as she made plans to leave her husband, she met Tom Lowery again.

The DC sent to Witham station returned with the information that a man fitting Millson's description of him had alighted there from the London-bound train the morning of last Thursday week.

'He was very noticeable—apart from his blue hat and haversack,' the DC explained, 'because it was a commuter train and he was the only person to get off. Everyone else was scrambling to get on.'

Millson immediately summoned a press conference and told reporters it was believed Philip Richmond was somewhere in East Anglia, possibly in the Colchester area. He was now wearing a blue baseball cap and carrying a blue haversack.

'And he may have darkened his hair and no longer be wearing glasses,' Millson added. 'The police urgently need help in tracing him and anyone with information should contact the Incident Room or any police station.'

*

When Scobie returned from Tendring Millson brought him up to date. 'Richmond didn't travel to London. He doubled back on his tracks and he's hiding up somewhere in this area. I've put out another appeal for information.'

'You don't think his wife's in on this? Covering up for him?'

Millson snorted. 'No chance! As you said yourself, she doesn't care for him one little bit. She certainly wouldn't help him escape arrest. How did you fare with your land research?'

'Would you believe? Melissa Richmond owns that plot. So she could be behind the sabotage. And if Lowery's her lover, as Mrs Pearson says, he could be doing the dirty work. I mean, what could be easier for him? He knows the yard inside out and he's on his own there every other night. How d'you fancy him as a suspect?'

'I don't. Not without some direct evidence,' Millson said. 'But I think we should ask Mrs Richmond about that piece of land.'

Melissa attended her aunt's funeral with her mother. She dissuaded Philip from accompanying her because his presence at her aunt's cottage would have intruded on a treasured memory.

While she was waiting for the hearse to arrive Melissa walked down the garden. It was overgrown and neglected now, but the summer-house was still there at the bottom. She went inside and looked out through the latticed window where she'd kept watch for her aunt as Tom Lowery made love to her.

At the cemetery, as her aunt's coffin was lowered into the grave, Melissa briefly raised her eyes and was startled to see Tom Lowery staring intently at her from behind a group of mourners. As their eyes met, a throb of emotion jolted Melissa like an electric shock and she hurriedly lowered her eyes again.

As soon as the interment ended she walked over to him. 'What are you doing here, Tom?' His frank appraisal of her womanhood sent quivers through her.

'I was fond of the old girl and she were of me.'

The voice, less coarse now, stirred her as it had then. She remembered teasing him over it, flaunting her high-school accent.

Swiftly, they bridged the years for each other. She spoke of her marriage to Philip and he of his divorce and his job as a welder at Tanniford's shipyard.

While the mourners ate and drank in the cottage parlour after the funeral, Melissa slipped down the garden to the summer-house. He was there, waiting. Four years of un-satisfactory marriage had left her starved and dry and when he lifted her black skirt she almost fainted with excitement. Instinctively, she turned her head to keep watch out of the lattice window as she'd done all those years ago.

At Melissa Richmond's house in Findlesham Millson came straight to the point. 'I understand you own some land adjacent to the shipyard which is vital to the development plan.'

Her eyes flashed and then she smiled frostily. 'My, you have been digging around, Chief Inspector. Yes, I own that land. What of it?'

'You seem to have kept your ownership very secret.'

She smiled crookedly. 'Oh come, Chief Inspector. I'm sure you realize the information is commercially sensitive. Besides which, wild horses wouldn't make Nicola sell the yard if she found out it would make me rich. She'd find some way to prevent it. Why are the police interested in this?'

'We've had reports of damage to machinery and equip-ment in the shipyard. Miss Richmond thinks the intention is to delay the launch of the ship and put her in financial difficulties so she'll be forced to sell the yard to Mr Hartman.'

'What has that to do with me?'

'Don't play simple with me, Mrs Richmond,' Millson said tartly. 'You know very well that would result in Mr Hartman taking up his option to buy your land for a large sum of money. Five hundred thousand pounds, I believe.'

'I see.' Melissa Richmond's eyes narrowed. 'Are you implying that *I* have something to do with those attacks, then?' she asked coldly. 'Because if you are, it's ridiculous! The shareholders' meeting will vote to sell to Hartman, anyway, whatever Nicola thinks. Philip will make sure of that.'

'You mean he's going to vote against her?' Scobie asked in surprise.

'Yes. He'll be doing the other shareholders a favour.'

'I find it hard to believe he'd betray his own daughter,' Scobie said. 'And I understood she gave him the shares on the understanding he'd always vote as she did.'

Melissa smiled cynically. 'Money changes minds, Sergeant.'

'You mean your husband knows about your land deal?' Millson asked.

'No, I mean he will do quite well out of the sale of his shares. They all will, including Nicola.'

'But you're the one who gains most of all if the yard is sold,' Millson said.

'Yes!' She spat the word through her teeth. 'And so I should! By right that shipyard should have been Philip's, not hers. She ruined my life.' Melissa's eyes glowed with hate. 'She seduced that old man into leaving the yard to her. You should have seen them together. He was always touching her . . . tweaking . . . and she—'

Millson interrupted the flow of invective. 'Does your husband know of your affair with Mr Lowery?'

The question threw her. Her mouth sagged.

After their reunion Tom Lowery had given up his welding job. He transferred to a night security post at the yard and bought a houseboat on Roman river a short walk from Melissa's house in Findlesham. She'd then engaged him as a part-time gardener to provide an excuse for him to call there when Philip was out.

Melissa recovered herself and said angrily, 'I suppose some gossip told you that. No, Philip doesn't know about Tom, though I don't see what business it is of yours. I shall tell him after my land's sold. Then he can divorce me.'

'And you still expect him to return for the shareholders' meeting on Wednesday?'

She seemed to consider the question. 'On reflection, maybe not.'

'Oh? Why do you say that?'

'Philip is a coward where his daughter's concerned. He'd be scared to face her across the table and vote against her. So it wouldn't surprise me if he stayed away. That would have the same result. She'd lose the vote without his fifteen per cent.'

'Why didn't you tell us this before?'

'Disclose my hand and risk losing half a million? You must be joking!' she said derisively.

'She's devious, that girl,' Millson said as the front door closed behind them. 'She varies her story like a chameleon changes colour so you hardly notice it.'

'You don't believe her?'

'No. She looks me straight in the eye all the time.' Millson smiled wryly. 'Only senior officers and hardened criminals do that. I think she's lying about Richmond letting his daughter down. She only said that to convince us there was no reason for her and Lowery to sabotage the yard. Let's ask Lowery what he was doing the night Janet West was killed. Where does he live?'

'Handy actually. On a houseboat just down the road here.'

'*Very* handy,' said Millson. 'For them both.'

The houseboat, a converted Thames sailing barge, lay in a creek that was almost land-locked where Roman river joined the Colne opposite Tanniford.

Following Scobie's directions, Millson drove down the dead-end road from Findlesham and turned on to a muddy track across the marshland. At the end of the track the superstructure of the houseboat could be seen above the riverbank. He brought the car to a halt on a patch of clinker near the bank where the rear of a red Audi protruded from a shed.

The scrunch of tyres on the clinker brought Lowery out on deck. There was no surprise on his face as they walked up the gangway. Millson saw the mobile phone clipped to Lowery's belt and guessed Melissa Richmond had fore-warned him.

Lowery led them below into a spacious lounge that occu-pied half the original hold of the vessel. 'Take your pick,' he said, indicating an assortment of easy chairs and drop-ping into one himself.

They sat down. 'Where were you on the evening of last Wednesday week, Mr Lowery?' Millson asked.

'The night that woman was murdered, you mean? I was in the pub up the road here. The Three Bottles. It's me local.'

'All evening?'

'No, I come back here for 'bout an hour and a half to watch a Western on telly. 'D'you want the exact times?'

'It would help.'

'I got to the pub at half eight, had a couple of beers and left just afore nine. I come back here, watched telly till ten-thirty then went back to the pub and stayed there till closing time.' Lowery gazed confidently at Scobie busily writing down the times. 'You can check with the pub.'

'Oh, we will,' Millson said. 'Thank you for your time.' He clambered up the companionway to the deck.

The barman at the Three Bottles readily confirmed the times of Lowery's comings and goings.

'How can you be so sure?' Scobie asked. 'It was nearly a fortnight ago.'

'I wanted to watch the same film as Tom, but the guv'nor insisted we had the European Cup match on in the bar. It was *The Gunfighter*, with Gregory Peck. Tom left just before it came on and was back soon after it finished.'

Millson bought two beers and carried them to a table. 'Could Lowery have driven to Tanniford and back in an hour and a half?' he asked Scobie.

'I shouldn't think so. And if he did, he certainly wouldn't have had time to murder Janet West, wheel her body along the river and return the barrow to the yard.'

'You'd better check it anyway,' Millson said.

On the waterfront at Tanniford that night, a figure in dark blue overalls and a balaclava flitted from the shadow of a passageway between the cottages. The passageway led from the side of the Black Dog, past the rear of Page's House where the pianist, Semprini, had once lived and along the back gardens of cottages to the riverfront.

After a glance up and down the deserted quay, the man turned and padded towards the shipyard. Keeping to the shadows, he crossed the end of the wet dock and continued between the tall corrugated shed and the paint shop into the yard.

He paused for a moment to accustom his eyes to the deeper blackness where the hull of *Vivacity* blotted out what little starlight there was, then followed the length of the hull to its stern at the water's edge. Under the stern, where the concrete apron sloped down into the river, a timber

cradle had been erected in preparation for the launching.
There was a similar cradle under the bow. The cradles
would keep the hull upright and prevent it careering to one
side when the dog-shores were knocked away and the ship
began her slide into the water.

The man took a flexible wire saw from the pocket of his
overalls and clambered into the framework of the cradle.
Wedging himself between two uprights, he began quietly
sawing at one of the cross-members.

Former constable Mike Kitchin took his night security job
very seriously. Any further sabotage would have disastrous
consequences for the yard, Nicola Richmond had explained, and he intended to make sure none occurred while
he was on duty.

Strictly against regulations, he'd retained his truncheon
when he retired. He simply handed in another one he'd
kept when he transferred from the Metropolitan police to
the Essex constabulary. The familiar hardness down the
inside of his regulation trousers—also retained on retire-
ment—was reassuring.

Unlike Leonard Pearson, he varied the time of his
rounds, knowing from experience that criminals more often
than not relied on their victims following a regular timetable. Tonight, instead of beginning the second round at
eleven o'clock, he'd set out an hour earlier at ten.

At the launching cradle, the intruder had made a thin saw
cut half way through the cross-member and then repeated
the process with a second timber. Using a small brush and
with the aid of a pencil torch, he brushed away the fine
sawdust that had fallen on the frame. He directed the tiny
beam of light at the timbers and examined the saw cuts.
They were almost invisible. In the mouth aperture of the
balaclava, his teeth gleamed in a malicious smile.

Although the hull needed only modest support to keep

it upright as it gathered momentum on its slide into the water, these weakened timbers would fracture as the weight of the hull came on them and one side of the cradle would collapse. The unstable hull would skew off the launchways and on to the concrete apron instead of entering the water. The damage would be considerable and the problems and cost of re-launching a three-thousand-ton vessel half in and half out of the water were enormous.

Mike Kitchin's sharp ears detected the faint sounds made by the man and he crept towards them, drawing his truncheon and holding a flashlight at the ready. He was too old a hand to rush into an unknown situation. He waited, patiently identifying the sounds and assessing how many intruders he had to deal with. Satisfied it was only one, he stepped forward as the man climbed off the cradle. Switching on his searchlight torch, he bellowed in a stentorian voice.

'Stay where you are! This is a citizen's arrest!'

He didn't expect the culprit to obey. The warning was a necessary formality to be observed before taking further action. The man froze for a second, then started to run, as Mike Kitchin had expected. He raised his truncheon and as the intruder darted to one side to pass him, he brought it down smartly on the man's shoulder close to the neck. The man gasped with pain and lurched sideways, the muscles on one side of his body temporarily paralysed. The ex-policeman raised the truncheon again and struck with controlled force in the same place on the other shoulder. The man staggered groggily, then buckled at the knees. Kitchin pushed him into a prostrate position on the ground, whipped a pair of handcuffs from his pocket and swiftly cuffed his wrists.

'Now, let's have a look at you.' Turning his prisoner over, he pulled off the balaclava and shone the torch on his face.

CHAPTER 18

Millson received the call from Scobie as he was finishing breakfast.

'The ex-copper Miss Richmond took on as Pearson's replacement caught an intruder in the yard last night.' Scobie sounded exultant. 'It's the man who's been doing the damage all right.'

'Who is he?'

'This'll surprise you. Ronald Stebbing . . . Laura's husband. Kitchin caught him sawing away at the launching cradle. They're holding him at Colchester nick on a charge of causing malicious damage.'

'I'll join you there in half an hour.'

'I've just spoken to Miss Richmond,' Scobie said as he and Millson walked along the corridor to the interview room. 'She gave me an ear-bashing over what you said again yesterday to the media about her father. She's worked out that we have evidence of her father's presence in the rest-room and says it must be from the time he called on her a month ago. She says he became unwell and lay down on the bed for a while.'

'Well, she would say that, wouldn't she?' Millson said, unimpressed. 'What d'you speak to her for?'

'To confirm the dates of the previous incidents with her.'

'I'm only interested in the night of the murder and whether this man's our killer,' Millson said. 'Someone else can follow up the malicious damage charge.'

'Well, I also asked her about Stebbing, because his wife told us he used to work at the yard. Miss Richmond says he was employed as a cashier and she sacked him three months ago for fiddling the books.'

Millson's face brightened. 'Good work, Norris. We'll start with that and work our way round to Janet West.'

A surly Ronald Stebbing stared at the tape-recorder. He was still wearing overalls. Underneath, the open neck of his shirt was dirty. Millson dictated the time and date and the particulars of the interview and reminded him he was still under caution.

'What were you doing in the shipyard last night?' Millson began.

'I'm saying nothing,' Stebbing answered.

Scobie leaned forward. 'You used to work there, didn't you?'

Stebbing's mouth closed obstinately.

'And you were sacked for fiddling the books,' Millson said.

'That's a lie!' Stebbing snarled. 'They didn't prove a thing. She'd no right to sack me.'

'Miss Richmond, you mean?' Scobie asked. 'Then why didn't you appeal to an industrial tribunal against unfair dismissal?'

His lip curled. 'She said if I did that she'd bring charges. She had me by the balls.'

'You were pretty angry about it, then?' Millson asked.

'Yes, I bloody was! Twelve years I worked there and got kicked out with a month's wages. Not a penny redundancy!' Stebbing said venomously.

'So you decided to take revenge,' Scobie said, continuing Millson's theme. 'You vandalized equipment and machinery so the schedule would be disrupted and Miss Richmond would lose money.'

'She deserved it. Her with all her money and me with nothing.'

'You admit the offence, then?'

'I was caught, wasn't I?' Stebbing said aggressively. 'I'm going to spill a bibful about her, I can tell you. She'd no right to do what she did. She had no evidence and I'm—'

Millson cut him off. 'You can state your case in court, Stebbing. I want to ask you about something else. Do you know a Mrs Richmond? Mrs Melissa Richmond?'

Stebbing frowned. 'No.'

'Are you quite sure?'

''Course I'm sure.'

'And where were you on the evening of last Wednesday week?'

'What's that got to do with anything?' Stebbing asked suspiciously. 'That's the night of the murder.'

'Just answer the question, please,' Millson insisted.

'I was playing darts at my local in Weeley. I always play darts Wednesday evening.'

'Plenty of people to confirm that then, are there?'

Stebbing hesitated. 'Well . . . yes.' His aggression had suddenly evaporated. 'Why? I had nothing to do with that woman's death. I didn't even know her—except as some woman who worked with my wife.'

Scobie opened his notebook. 'What time did you go to the pub that evening?'

'Why? I told you—'

'Answer the question!' Millson snapped. 'We want to know what time you went there . . . when you left . . . and the names of the people who can vouch for you.'

Stebbing's eyes slewed sideways. 'I'm not saying anything more till I speak to a solicitor.'

'Very well. Interview suspended at—' Millson consulted his watch—'ten-fifteen.' He flicked the switch of the tape-recorder.

WDC Tracey Bennett was certain that when she'd interviewed ten-year-old Jimmy Monk he'd been on the brink of telling her something. But his father came into the room and Jimmy clammed up. Tracey knew the boy didn't take school dinners and went home for his meal so she decided to waylay him as he came out of school in the lunch break.

'Hallo, Jimmy. Would you like a lift?' She'd parked by the school gates.

'Yes, please.' He jumped in.

Without starting the car, she said, 'I believe you were going to tell me something the other evening, Jimmy. What was it?'

He was silent, staring ahead through the windscreen. 'Are you afraid of what your dad will say?'

He flinched and she realized what the problem was. 'Have you done something you shouldn't? Something your dad would be cross about?'

He nodded. Tracey was nineteen with no experience of children. What sort of mischief did a timid ten-year-old get up to? She couldn't imagine it being anything terrible, although it might seem so to him.

'Jimmy, listen to me. A lady has been killed—a nice lady like your mum. If you know anything—anything at all—you must tell me.'

'It wasn't anything really,' he said.

'Let me decide that.'

'Dad'll give me a hiding.'

'I know a man who'll see he doesn't,' she said firmly.

His face turned towards her. 'Yeh? Who?'

'He's called Chief Inspector Millson,' she said. 'And he frightens everyone, including me.'

'Yeh?' He sounded interested. 'What's he like, then?'

Tracey Bennett took a breath and in the line of duty gave a thoroughly unflattering description of George Millson, Actually, she rather liked him. When she came to the hair on the back of his hands, Jimmy was impressed.

'Get away!'

'Oh yes,' Tracey said, 'thick and black. He'd terrify your dad.'

'OK, can I speak to *him*, then?'

*

The interview with Ronald Stebbing resumed at twelve-fifteen. The solicitor was a small man in glasses, wearing a dog-tooth suit and with straight brown hair brushed off his forehead.

'I take it the questions you wish to put to my client are in connection with some other offence, not the one of causing malicious damage with which he has been charged,' he said.

Millson wasn't falling for that one. If he answered 'Yes, the killing of Janet West,' the solicitor would probably advise Stebbing not to answer further questions at this stage. And Millson wasn't ready to charge him with murder . . . yet.

'On the contrary,' Millson said. 'I have reason to believe he committed the same offence on other dates, including the night of Wednesday the fourteenth of April.'

The solicitor looked disappointed. 'I just wanted to get that clear,' he said. He cleared his throat. 'My client was not present in the public house for the whole of the evening. He left for a while and returned later.'

The same excuse as Lowery? Millson wondered. 'Nipped back home to watch a programme on telly, did he?' he asked sceptically.

The solicitor looked surprised. 'Er—no.'

'I went for a drive,' Stebbing said. He sounded confident.

'Where?'

'Round the villages. Torrington . . . Thorpe . . . Kirby . . .'

'What for?'

'Boggling.'

'Boggling,' Millson said heavily. 'You mean peeping. You're admitting to being a Peeping Tom?'

'That's right.' Stebbing had a smug expression on his face.

'And there were no witnesses, of course,' Millson said sourly.

'That's right.'

Millson snapped at the microphone, 'Interview suspended at twelve-twenty!' He switched off the tape-recorder and addressed the solicitor. 'A word with you outside.'

In the corridor he said angrily, 'This is just a fairy tale to cover him for the time of the murder.'

'Chief Inspector, I understood the questions were only to be about malicious damage, the offence for which he was arrested,' the solicitor said smoothly.

'Do you want me to charge him with murder and caution him before I resume the interview, then?' Millson challenged.

The solicitor was unperturbed. 'I don't think you even have grounds for suspicion.'

'Oh, but I do. The dead woman has left all her money— a sizeable amount, I may say—to his wife, so he benefits handsomely from her death, albeit indirectly. And he's admitted attacking the shipyard because of a grudge, so he could well have been there Wednesday night when she was murdered.'

The solicitor looked worried as Millson went on, 'Now, if he's telling the truth about his movements, we *might* be able to substantiate them, provided he gives us details of the girls and the locations. Otherwise, I shall assume he's made up this Peeping Tom story.'

'Very well. I'll speak to him,' the solicitor said.

When Tracey Bennett collected Jimmy Monk after lunch he was a mixture of bravado and trepidation. 'Am I being taken in for questioning?'

'No. Your mum's agreed we can ask you questions, but you don't have to answer any you don't want to. And she'll write a note to your teacher so you won't get in trouble for being absent from school.'

At the resumed interview, Ronald Stebbing provided locations, times and descriptions of the young girls he'd spied on.

'Prefer them very young, do you?' Millson asked, keeping his tone neutral. Laura Stebbing was right to leave this man. He was a toad.

'Not particularly,' Stebbing said, unconcerned. 'They go to bed earlier. The bigger chicks don't start undressing till later.'

Millson told him the information would be checked and if he was satisfied his story was correct he'd probably be charged with causing a breach of the peace.

'And if I'm not satisfied that's what you were doing,' he said, 'I shall detain you for questioning about the murder of Janet West.'

That, he was pleased to see, wiped the smug expression from Stebbing's face. Meantime, Millson decided, he would apply for Stebbing to be remanded in custody. Laura deserved a break.

'Think he's telling the truth?' Scobie asked Millson after the interview.

'I don't know. He could be fobbing us off with his activities on a previous Wednesday evening . . . same times, same locations, same girls. It'll be difficult to prove he *wasn't* peeping that Wednesday.'

Scobie glanced at the clock. 'Lunch?' When they were in Colchester he and Millson usually lunched in the Red Lion.

Millson was perusing a note on his desk. 'No, you go ahead. Something's come up. I have to talk to a Brussels sprout.'

'A what?' Scobie asked.

Millson sighed. 'A Brussels sprout is a boy scout, Norris, at least it was when I was a lad. It's rhyming slang.'

'He won't eat you,' WDC Bennett told Jimmy Monk, leading him towards a blue Sierra as it drove into the shipyard car park.

Jimmy wasn't so sure about that when he came face to

face with the fearsome-looking Millson a moment later.
And if Tracey Bennett hadn't looked like his favourite aunt,
whom he loved and trusted, he would have turned and fled.

He felt slightly less anxious when Millson produced a
large bag of sweets from his pocket and handed them to
him as he clambered into the back of the car with Tracey
Bennett. And when the Chief Inspector took a sandwich
from a plastic container and began eating, Jimmy knew he
was safe.

'My lunch,' Millson explained, chewing away. Unhur-
riedly, he chatted to the boy and steered the conversation
round to the last scout meeting. Jimmy Monk hardly
noticed he was answering questions as he responded to
Millson's prompting.

On his way home after the scout meeting, and against
his father's orders, Jimmy had detoured to the chip shop
in East Street with two of his mates.

'My dad'll belt me when he finds out,' Jimmy said.

'No, he won't,' Millson said. 'Not after I've spoken to
him.'

Jimmy looked at the hands tearing open a plastic bag
containing fruit. 'He's got long hairs on the back of his
hands like a gorilla,' he informed his goggle-eyed com-
panions later. At the moment they convinced young Jimmy
Monk this man could protect him from his father's wrath,
so he went on, 'We hung around outside the shop gassing
and chomping for a bit, then the others went off up the
High Street and I walked home past the shipyard.'

Scobie's phone rang soon after he returned from the Red
Lion.

'Pick up Goodman!' Millson barked in his ear. 'If he
doesn't come voluntarily arrest him on suspicion of murder.
I'm on my way back.'

CHAPTER 19

Kevin Goodman's normally pink cheeks were pale and he looked anxious as he faced Millson and Scobie in the interview room. He blinked when Millson shot the first question at him.

'Why did you tell us you didn't go through the shipyard after the scout meeting? We have a witness who saw you coming out of the yard at ten o'clock.'

Jimmy Monk, making his way home along Spring Street, had been surprised to see his scoutmaster come out of the shipyard and hurry up Anglesea Road ahead of him. He'd looked at his watch, wondering why Mr Goodman was so late.

Goodman's eyes darted from Millson to Scobie and back again. He said nervously, 'I didn't want to be involved. The newspapers said the body had been found by the path and she'd been killed about nine-thirty. That was the time I was walking along there.'

'So you didn't take a short cut across the field? You walked home through the shipyard?'

Goodman swallowed. 'Yes.'

'And is the rest of your story a lie too?'

'No. Everything else I told you was true.'

Millson, noting the man's increasing nervousness, remained silent for a while. At last he said,

'I'll tell you what I think. I think Janet kept that nine-thirty appointment with you and you had a quarrel . . . maybe she threatened to tell your wife unless you paid her more money. You killed her, put her body in that wheelbarrow on the barge, wheeled it along the path and dumped it half way to the shipyard. Then you took the money and credit cards from her handbag, scattered the rest around to make it look like a mugging and returned the wheel-barrow to the barge. After which you walked back along the path and through the yard to your home.' Millson put his hands behind his head and leaned back in his chair. 'What d'you say to that?'

Goodman said in a tight voice, 'I say it's completely untrue. If I'd killed her, I'd run home across the fields, wouldn't I? Why would I risk walking back past her body?'

Millson's hands came from behind his head and slapped the table. 'To make sure she was dead, of course.'

Goodman gazed at him, wide-eyed. 'That's not true!'

'Why *did* you, then? Go through the shipyard, I mean?'

'I always go home that way at this time of year. I only use the field in summer when it's light.'

Scobie said, 'That's not what you told us when we questioned you before. You said you went across the field because you were in a hurry to get home before your wife.'

'Yes, well I've explained why I said that,' Goodman mumbled.

Millson said harshly, 'You had opportunity, motive and the means to move the body. And you've lied about your movements. Now let's have the truth!'

'I've told you the truth,' Goodman said desperately. 'Janet didn't come to the barge that night . . . we didn't meet . . . and I didn't kill her!' His voice was shaking.

Millson's voice was relentless. 'You've already lied to me twice. You said you didn't know her and you said you walked home across the field. And now you say you didn't kill her. Why should I believe you?'

Goodman lowered his head and said nothing.

Millson went on, 'You admit to being close to where her body was found at the time she was killed. Now, if you didn't kill her, then someone else did and he was there—with a wheelbarrow—at the same time as you. So, why didn't you see him?'

'I don't know!' Goodman's head lifted. 'Because it was dark, I suppose.'

'I find that unbelievable,' Millson said.

He waited and when Goodman made no response, he continued, 'I'd like you to accompany me to the barge and explain exactly what your movements were that night. Are you prepared to do that?'

Goodman nodded.

He was driven to Tanniford in a police car, Millson and Scobie following.

'He could be telling the truth,' Scobie said as they drove down the hill into Tanniford. 'We don't know when the body was put there. It could have been later, after Goodman passed.'

'I realize that,' Millson said. 'But he hasn't suggested it and I'm not going to. I'm certain he's hiding something and I want to find out what it is.'

At the shipyard a constable stayed with the cars and another accompanied Goodman as he followed Millson and Scobie. They walked through the yard under the gaze of men attaching heavy drug chains to the ship in preparation for tomorrow's launch.

Millson led the way through the gate on to the riverbank and trudged along the path to the scout barge. Standing at the foot of the gangplank, he asked Goodman, 'What time did you start walking home from here?'

'A quarter to ten. I'd given Janet a quarter of an hour and decided not to wait any longer.'

'Right. You can start walking and I want you to do exactly as you did then. Sergeant Scobie will keep a note of the time.'

'All right.' Goodman set off along the path trailed by Scobie, Millson and the constable. 'It was dark, of course,' he said over his shoulder. 'And quiet—I remember I could hear the lap of water along the bank. It makes sucking noises in the mud as the tide rises.'

After a short distance, Scobie, who was methodically pacing the steps, checked his watch. 'You've only covered fifty yards in a minute,' he said. 'It should be seventy-five at a normal walking pace of two and a half miles an hour.'

'Unless you were wheeling a barrow, of course,' Millson commented.

Goodman stopped and stared at them with a frightened expression. 'I—I didn't realize you were timing me.'

'Time is what this is all about,' Millson told him. 'You remember whether you were dawdling or hurrying, don't you?'

'Yes, I was walking normally.'

'On you go, then.'

Goodman stepped off more briskly. He glanced sideways as they passed the place where Janet West's body had lain. The only sign of the activity a fortnight ago was a rectangular patch of flattened grass around the area that had been cordoned off.

'Four minutes,' Scobie announced as Goodman opened the iron gate into the shipyard. On the far side, beneath the bow of *Vivacity*, workmen were erecting a platform for the naming ceremony.

Goodman turned and followed the right of way. 'I remember there were lights in the administration block and in the office at the entrance,' he said. 'And also a blue light in a porthole in the middle of the ship. A neon, I suppose, because it was flickering.'

He continued walking towards the entrance. Millson stopped him when he reached the place where Jimmy Monk had first seen him.

Scobie checked his watch. 'Six minutes from the barge to here.'

Millson nodded to the constable accompanying them. 'Take him back now.'

*

At the resumed questioning in the interview room, Millson said, 'If you left the barge at nine-forty-five, you should have reached the shipyard exit by nine-fifty-one. The witness saw you hurrying out of there at ten o'clock. That leaves nine minutes unaccounted for.'

'I don't see how you can be that precise. It was dark and I may have walked more slowly and—'

'You're lying!' Millson said angrily.

Goodman flinched and dropped his eyes. His hands were clenched together on the table, the knuckles showing white.

Millson said in a stern voice, 'You do realize the seriousness of your position, don't you, Goodman?'

'Yes.' He answered in a whisper.

'Then I urge you to tell me the truth. What were you doing during that time?'

Goodman unclenched his hands, ran a finger round the inside of his collar and clasped his hands together again. They were shaking now. 'I was looking for Janet—I thought she might be with Pearson.'

'Why should you think that?'

'When she was late once before, she made a joke about having to pay him a toll for passing through the yard. I think he knew why she came to the barge and he was making her . . . well . . . go and see him first. She even had to wear sexy underwear to please him.'

'And did you find them together?'

'No. I looked in the administration block windows and his office by the entrance, but there was no sign of either of them.'

Millson scratched his chin, considering another possibility. The absence of a suicide note together with the lack of a reason for Pearson to kill himself, bothered Millson.

'Where were you last Thursday night? Between ten o'clock and midnight, say?'

'At home,' Goodman said, looking surprised.

'You didn't go out at all?'

'Only to take the dog for a walk.'

'How long did that take?'

'About half an hour. Why?' Goodman's eyes widened. 'That was the night Pearson committed suicide! Here, what are you suggesting?'

'You implied Pearson was taking advantage of Janet and knew why she came to see you. Was he blackmailing you?'

'No! Anyway, he committed suicide, didn't he?'

'The inquest hasn't been held yet,' Millson said. 'We found Janet West's diary in his pocket. Perhaps *you* put it there to incriminate him, then killed him and faked the death to look like suicide.'

'Of course I didn't, I didn't go near the shipyard Thursday night!' Goodman's voice rose hysterically. 'I'm not answering any more questions. I came here voluntarily. Are you going to detain me? If so, I want a solicitor.'

'No, that's all for the moment,' Millson said. 'You're free to leave. Keep yourself available for further questions, though.'

'You'll have to arrest me next time,' Goodman said defiantly.

Later on Tuesday afternoon, a woman phoned the Incident Room in response to the revised description of Philip Richmond that Millson had issued to the Press yesterday. She reported seeing a man like that getting into a white Mercedes outside Witham station on the morning of Thursday 15th April.

'It was about nine o'clock,' she said, 'I was walking past the station on my way to work.'

No, she hadn't seen who was driving the car she told the constable who took her call.

Scobie relayed the report to Millson. 'Melissa Richmond owns a white Mercedes,' Scobie pointed out. 'It was standing in the garage the first time we went there. I suppose it's just coincidence, though she did say she drove her husband to the station Thursday morning. What if—?' He stopped. 'No, that's absurd. Why would Mrs Richmond put her husband on the train at Colchester and pick him up again at Witham, disguised as someone else?'

Millson's eyes had glazed over, a sign he was in deep thought. Scobie waited to see if some startling revelation would follow this intense concentration. It did.

Millson came out of his daze and thumped his fist on the table.

'I've been seeing this the wrong way round, Norris! It wasn't Philip Richmond disguised as someone else who left the train at Witham. Richmond never got on the train at Colchester. It was someone pretending to be him. Someone who changed back to himself in the toilet and got off at Witham. Someone who wanted to establish that Richmond caught a train to London that morning.'

'Who?' Scobie asked.

'Lowery,' Millson said. 'It wasn't difficult. He's dark-haired and he's the same build. A dash of talcum powder in his hair, Richmond's clothes and glasses . . . and the initialled travel bag, of course.'

Scobie gaped at him. 'But why?'

'Because Richmond refused to vote against his daughter and Melissa Richmond was going to lose half a million pounds. They've killed him, Norris! Philip Richmond isn't trotting around the country collecting antique mugs. He's dead! We've got another murder on our hands.'

CHAPTER 20

On Wednesday, the day of the launch, the weather was mild and there was barely a breath of wind. It was a relief to the watermen. Launchings at Tanniford were tricky because the river was narrow. If the drag chains weren't heavy enough, the vessel would shoot across the river and embed her stern in the opposite bank. And if they were too heavy, she would launch slowly and end up half in and half out of the water. The worst hazard, though, was a strong wind. As soon as the unballasted hull was afloat on the water the wind could blow it sideways, making it almost impossible for the tractors to haul the ship round into the wet dock.

The invitations to the launching ceremony had been sent out the previous week. Except for one. Andrew Hartman was surprised to receive an invitation that morning. DO PLEASE COME was written across it in a bold feminine hand.

He sat at his desk, holding the card between thumb and forefinger and tapping it against the palm of his other hand. He came to a decision and, leaning forward, depressed the switch on the intercom. 'What engagements do I have to-day, Gilda?'

'The managing director of Perry's is coming to see you at twelve o'clock and you're lunching with the Chamber of Commerce at one, Mr Hartman.'

'Cancel them both,' Hartman ordered. His mouth curved in a smile. 'I'm going to see a ship being launched.'

Gilda Flemming was too well-trained to comment upon her boss accepting a last-minute invitation like this. She was curious to know who'd sent it. Whoever she was, Gilda thought, the lady must have powerful appeal for Andrew

Hartman to give her precedence over two important business engagements.

The invitation that arrived at Melissa's house a week earlier had been addressed to Mr & Mrs Philip Richmond. In the past, launching ceremonies had served only to remind Melissa of her grievance against the Richmond family and she'd declined to attend them. This was one she wouldn't miss for the world, though. She set the card prominently on the Welsh dresser and stretched her arms above her head with a contented sigh.

So much had changed in the year since Aunt Harriet's funeral. She had a wonderful lover and she was going to be very, very rich. It was Tom who'd opened her eyes to the potential of Auntie's little plot of land, even before the solicitors had obtained probate, let alone registered her ownership with the Land Registry.

To Poulson Bannerman who executed the will she'd been simply: 'issue of Jack Bridewell'—her dead father—and she'd only had to produce her birth certificate to prove it. She hadn't told them she was married or where she lived.

When she discovered how much Andrew Hartman was willing to pay for the plot, she continued to conceal her identity and the solicitors had negotiated the contract with Andrew Hartman's company as 'executors of the late Harriet Bridewell'. Melissa intended no one except Tom to know of her land deal until the day it exploded in Nicola's face.

Scobie took the slip road off the A12 to Kelvedon and then the turning to Tiptree.

'When was the last time we know for certain Richmond was alive?' Millson had asked yesterday.

'The neighbour we spoke to said she caught a glimpse of him leaving the house in his car about eight o'clock Wednesday evening,' Scobie reminded him.

'But can we be sure it was Richmond? If Lowery imper-
sonated him Thursday morning, he might have done so
Wednesday evening as well.'

'Well, the only other information we have—' Scobie
turned back the pages of his notebook—'is that one of Richmond's clients spoke to him on the phone just after six
o'clock Wednesday evening, when the cheap rate started.
So Richmond was alive then.'

'Right. Then let's find out what Lowery and Mrs Richmond were doing from six o'clock onwards. Check with
that schoolfriend she said she spent the evening with. And
go over Lowery's story with him again. I still want to know
whether he could have got to Tanniford and back in the
time he was absent from the pub.'

'I don't see why. It wasn't him who was doing the damage to the yard, it was Stebbing.'

'Yes, but what bothers me is the coincidence of two
murders the same evening and in the same area, both
having connections with the shipyard. So double-check
his alibi.'

'OK. What'll you be doing?'

'Pursuing a light in the night,' Millson said.

Scobie waited for an explanation. Millson didn't offer
one. 'Off you go, Norris,' he said.

Melissa's schoolfriend, Julia Bamber, lived in a house
almost identical to Melissa's. She was a tall, dark-haired
girl and when she opened the door to Scobie her eyes
gave him the same predatory stare as Melissa's. Yes, she
agreed, Melissa was with her that evening from about
eight-thirty to eleven-thirty. They'd known each other
for years.

'Went to the same beastly school, you know,' she informed him in a drawling voice.

'What were relations like between her and her husband?'

She gave a wry smile. 'Cool.' She enunciated the word
with lips rounded in the shape of a kiss.

'Do you know a man called Thomas Lowery?'

'Her hunky gardener, you mean? No, but I wouldn't mind.' The smile became enigmatic.' Can't tell you a *thing* about him . . . or him and her . . . if that's what you're after.' Schoolgirl's honour and loyalty to old chums, her tone implied.

'You know we're trying to locate her husband?'

'Good Lord.' The grey eyes widened theatrically, showing the whites. 'Has he gone walkabout, then?'

'Haven't you seen the appeals for him in connection with the murder of Janet West?'

'Murders are so boring,' she said. 'There are so many of them these days. Quite honestly, I try to ignore them.'

'Was Mrs Richmond her usual self that evening?' Scobie asked.

'Oh yes. Absolutely.'

Julia Bamber watched Scobie walk down the path to his car. Melissa had chain-smoked all evening and guzzled G and Ts like they were lemonade while she waited for a phone call from Tom. When he phoned at half eleven, she fled home.

''Bye, sweetie,' Julia called from the door. But Melissa had gunned her car and scorched away like the Devil himself was after her.

'Naturally, I'm interested, poppet,' Julia said on the phone later when she heard the police were looking for Melissa's husband. Missy wouldn't talk about it, but Julia was sure she would confide in her eventually.

It was a shame she'd had to tell fibs to that honey of a policeman. A girl had to stand by her friends, though.

In her bedroom at Findlesham, Melissa Richmond put the finishing touches to her make-up and checked the result in the mirror. She glanced at her watch. No need to hurry. A late arrival would be more telling, especially as Nicola wasn't expecting her.

She paused in the act of applying more lipstick, her thoughts straying briefly to Philip . . . weak-kneed Philip, who wouldn't stand up to his daughter . . . wingeing about family loyalty.

'When she gave me those shares I promised I'd never vote against her.'

Melissa had tried to reason with him. 'The shares are practically worthless. Andrew Hartman is offering a very good price to buy you all out. Are you going to let Nicola prevent you and the other shareholders selling? Just so's she can hold on to her precious shipyard? You'll never get another chance like this.' She didn't add that neither would she get another chance to sell her land for half a million pounds.

'I gave my word,' he insisted.

'You're letting her ruin our lives again!' It was a repetition of what had happened with his father's will. She would be cheated yet again. Melissa's fury turned to cold-blooded decision.

'We have to kill him, Tom,' she told Lowery. 'It's the only way.'

Philip Richmond had been sitting at the desk in his study when she let Tom Lowery in through the kitchen door on Wednesday evening. Philip was peering at his VDU screen as Lowery stepped into the room behind him, wound a length of cord round his neck, then pulled it tight and knotted it.

Philip tumbled to the floor, frantically clawing the cord and managing to loosen it enough to breathe. Lowery kicked the chair aside and knelt astride his victim to finish him off. But Philip fought back vigorously. Lowery shouted for Melissa. She ran in, saw the two men struggling and picked up a cushion from one of the chairs.

'Hold his hands, Tom!'

Kneeling behind her husband's head, she put the cushion over his face and pressed down hard on it. In a moment or two his struggles weakened. She kept her weight on the cushion until he suffocated. It was half past seven.

There was no sign of Lowery when Scobie reached the houseboat. Nor of his red Audi. Scobie guessed he was at Tanniford watching the launch.

He wondered how he could check, let alone double-check, Lowery's alibi. He sauntered along the Roman river to the mill and continued to the bridge where a path led up to the car park at the rear of the Three Bottles. Lowery had walked to the pub as he always did, the barman had told them. That meant he'd have had to return to the houseboat for his car, which left even less time to drive to Tanniford and back.

Scobie returned to the houseboat now floating high on the rising tide. A dory with an outboard sitting on the transom was moored alongside. Lowery could have sped along the river to the pub and back in that, Scobie thought, but it would only have gained him a few minutes.

In the shipyard a crowd had begun to gather. The launch of a ship was a big occasion in Tanniford. Most of the village was there and all the shipyard workers and their families. The children had a day off from school and the pubs were open all day.

The foreman, Harry Tripp, anxiously checked the preparations. So many things could go wrong with a launch. The big yards had automatic systems that simultaneously triggered the release of the dog-shores and smashed the bottle of champagne against the bow at the press of a button. There was nothing fancy like that at Tanniford. Everything had to be done manually and be controlled by hand signals.

Across the yard he spotted the bulky figure of Chief Inspector Millson coming towards him and sighed. Aggravation was something he could do without at the moment.

'I'd like to go aboard and look over the ship,' Millson said.

Harry's jaw dropped. Of all the things Millson might have said, nothing could have caused him as much consternation as this.

'You can't. No one 'cept launching crew's allowed on now. She's going in in half an hour.'

'Not if you force me to arrest her, she isn't,' Millson said tersely.

Harry's jaw dropped even further, almost touching his collar. 'You can't arrest a ship!'

'Oh yes I can,' Millson said. 'If I think it holds vital evidence. You ask your Miss Richmond. Now . . .' He put an arm round Harry Tripp's shoulder. 'Why don't you come on board with me, Harry. I need your expertise.'

CHAPTER 21

On the platform beneath the bow of *Vivacity*, Sir Henry Wadham perused the notes for his speech. It was a proud day for Sir Henry who, in thirty years, had risen from East End scrap merchant to chairman of the company that had commissioned the building of the ship. The disposal of toxic waste was an expanding business and a bulk-carrier like the *Vivacity* was ideal for moving large quantities of it in safety.

He gazed anxiously at a placard being held up in the crowd. FOE, it read. Friends of the Earth, he supposed and hoped the environmentalists weren't going to make trouble. It comforted him to have seen uniformed police in the car park as he arrived in his Rolls.

It was a proud day too for his wife, Elsie, who sat beside him. She'd never launched a ship before and she felt like Royalty up here above the crowd in her new turquoise coat and dress. She'd had them made specially for the occasion and had chosen the colour with care after she'd asked her husband what colour the ship was painted.

'What the heck does it matter, Else?'

'I don't want my outfit to clash, you berk.' Elsie Wadham had Cockney origins like her husband.

Next to her, Nicola was worrying about the shareholders' meeting in an hour's time. The three other shareholders were here on the platform with their families. Where was her father? She couldn't believe he'd let her down. She caught Andrew Hartman's eye and smiled politely. She'd sent him the invitation on impulse, hoping he'd come and see for himself the industry and jobs his development plan would destroy. She was a little surprised he'd accepted, though.

A white Mercedes nudged its way into the crowded car park and found a place. Melissa stepped from it wearing a figure-hugging yellow dress and a picture hat with ribbon to match. She walked through the shipyard entrance and ascended the steps to the platform.

Nicola turned to see who the latecomer was and stared in amazement. Melissa gave her a wintry smile and took a seat beside Andrew Hartman.

On board *Vivacity* Millson and the foreman were in the midship section of her vast hold.

'Someone has told me there was a light inside the ship the night Janet West was murdered,' Millson said.

'What sort of light?' the foreman asked.

'He thought it was a neon because it was blue and it flickered.'

Harry Tripp shook his head. 'Sounds more like a welding torch to me.'

'Ahh . . . yes.' Millson let out a long sigh.

'Ain't no welding done here at night, though.'

'Uh-huh.' Millson looked around him. 'I don't see any portholes.'

'You don't have portholes in a ship's hold,' Harry said scathingly. 'Nearest one is in the passageway at the end there.'

Millson followed his pointing finger. Would the glare of a welding torch have seemed like a flickering neon tube to Kevin Goodman outside in the yard?

Millson gazed at the pristine paintwork of the hold, the neat lines of bolts in the floorplates. He began walking back and forth, methodically covering the floor section by section, watched by a mystified Harry Tripp.

At the end of one his perambulations Millson suddenly halted. He bent over, studying the floor then stooped and peered closer. Raising an arm, he beckoned the foreman.

*

Sir Henry Wadham stood up and stepped to the microphone. He began his speech with a tribute to the yard for completing on time.

'We'd have had fat penalty payments if they hadn't, of course,' he quipped, 'but we'd rather have the ship.'

Nicola smiled politely, wondering where the Chief Inspector and Sergeant Scobie were. She'd invited them and she was disappointed they weren't here.

With an anxious eye on the placard holder, Henry Wadham stressed the harmless nature of the cargoes the ship would carry. None of that nuclear stuff, he said, just hospital waste and the like. It had very, very, low levels of toxicity—not much more than the radiation from the sun or your television screen.

Millson indicated a circle of boltheads in the floor. 'These bolts have been interfered with. If you look closely you can see where the paint has been damaged.'

'They must've bin undone and done up again, then,' the foreman said. 'Can't think why.'

'What's under here?'

'Space. She's double-bottomed. It's taken up with buoyancy chambers and trimming tanks.'

'So what's this circle of bolts?'

'The trimming tanks have to be flooded or pumped out to keep the ship in trim when she's under way. That's an inspection plate over the pump and pipes.'

'I want it lifted,' Millson said.

The foreman made a face and unclipped the mobile phone from his belt. He spoke into it to someone called Terry and a few moments later Terry appeared carrying a bag of tools and a four-foot torque wrench. He unscrewed the bolts and hauled the circular plate aside. The rungs of an iron ladder led down into blackness.

The foreman lifted a lantern torch from the toolbag and descended the ladder. His muffled voice came back to them.

'Summat odd here, Inspector. You'd best take a look.'

Gingerly, Millson put his feet on the top rungs of the narrow ladder and lowered himself through the opening. There wasn't room to stand up between the outer hull and the floor of the hold and he had to bend double to step over the massive steel ribs of the ship and join the foreman. He was squatting against what appeared to be a steel wall.

Harry Tripp thumped the wall. 'This 'ere's a trimming tank. Look underneath.' He shone the torch.

Millson lay prone. One of the rectangular spaces between each pair of ribs and the bottom of the tank that rested on them had been blocked off by a steel plate.

'That shouldn't be there,' the foreman said, 'though only us as built her would know that.'

'Can you get it out?'

'Needs a blowtorch. It's bin spot-welded.'

Millson gave a satisfied nod. Now he understood why the light Goodman had seen was faint. It had been the distant reflection of a gas torch down here.

The foreman scrambled up the ladder followed by Millson. He rapped instructions to the workman, then looked at his watch.

'It's getting near time,' he said. 'I gotta go up top and see to things.'

'I'll stay here,' Millson said.

The foreman shook his head. 'Too dangerous. You'll be thrown the length of the hold when she goes in. You'll hit that bulkhead at the bottom there like you've fallen out a window a hundred foot up.'

Millson saw the workman, Terry, descending the ladder carrying a blow torch and wearing goggles. 'I'll go down there with him, then. I have to be present when he removes that steel plate.'

'Please yourself,' the foreman said.

*

Beneath the stern of the ship a waterman was watching the tide creeping up the concrete slope. It was his job to signal *l'heure de mer*, as the French termed it—the moment when the tide was at its highest and about to turn . . . the moment for launching. It was slack water now and for the last two minutes the water hadn't moved up or down.

Sir Henry was in full spate. He knew nothing about tides or the problems of launching a ship into a narrow river. He saw himself as a business tycoon. One of those who'd made it . . . 'Barrow-boy to baronet,' he told his friends inaccurately. His speech had several more paragraphs to run.

High above him in the bow of the ship, Harry Tripp saw the signal from the chief waterman in the stern, relaying the message from the waterman below him at the water's edge. Harry looked at his watch and swore quietly. An offshore wind at the estuary and low pressure had made the tide turn early.

He signalled to his man on the platform and drew a finger smartly across his throat. The man bent forward and whispered in Nicola's ear, 'Tide's turned, Miss.'

Nicola leaned sideways to Lady Wadham. 'We must launch within the next few minutes, Lady Wadham.'

Elsie Wadham tugged her husband's coat tail. 'Cut the cackle, Henry, and let me name the flippin' ship!'

As Sir Henry gabbled some closing words, men with sledge-hammers moved forward and awaited the signal to knock out the dog-shores—blocks of timber at intervals along the hull that held it steady on the keel blocks. At either side of the vessel tractors, with reels of cable attached to the bow, started their engines in readiness to snatch in cable if the ship entered the water too quickly and surged across the river to the opposite bank.

On the Findlesham side of the river Scobie strolled away from the houseboat to his car. On the other side of the river he could see the crowd in the shipyard and hear Sir Henry's speech clearly across the water. Scobie suddenly stopped. Turning about, he ran back towards the houseboat.

Lady Wadham rose to her feet. The chief waterman scissored his hands across his chest and the men with sledge-hammers began knocking out the dog-shores.

In the confined space beneath the floor of the hold, Terry extinguished the blowtorch and raised his goggles. Watched by Millson, he inserted a crowbar between the sheet of steelplate and the underside of the tank and began levering. As he did so he felt the hull beneath him tremble slightly. He dropped the crowbar and called urgently to Millson, 'She's going in! Get down between the ribs and brace yourself, guv'!'

In a fair imitation of Queen's English, Elsie Wadham's voice boomed through the public address system.

'I name this ship *Vivacity*! May God bless her and all who sail in her!'

She pulled a cord on the rail in front of her and a bottle of champagne swung forward in an arc and smashed against the hull. The crowd began cheering and simultaneously the last dog-shores were knocked away and the ship's bow slowly receded from the platform.

With gathering momentum, three thousand tons of steel slid down the launchways and plunged into the water with an enormous splash, sending shock waves up and down the river. Drag chains snaked out either side of the hull, slowing it down as it hit the water. The tractors revved engines and reeled in the slack on the bow cables and *Vivacity* came to rest, floating sedately.

Nicola closed her eyes in relief. A perfect lunch.

In the bowels of the ship, Terry picked up the crowbar and crawled forward to continue levering at the rectangle of steel. But the working of the hullplates under the tremendous strain of hitting the water had sprung it from position. It lay flat between the ribs.

'Torch, please, guv.'

Millson bent down and shone the torch into the cavity.

'Oh my God!' Terry breathed.

CHAPTER 22

As the tractors tightened in the bow lines and towed the ship to the wet dock where she would be fitted out, the platform party adjourned to Nicola's office for drinks and a buffet lunch.

A dory sped across the river with Scobie at the helm. He tied up at the concrete apron from where *Vivacity* had just been launched and walked along to the wet dock as the tractors finished coaxing the ship into her berth. He saw Millson descending the gangway and headed towards him.

Several police officers appeared from the other direction and hurried on board the vessel. They'd been summoned by Millson on the foreman's mobile phone.

'What's going on?' Scobie asked Millson.

'Richmond's body was welded up in the bottom of the ship. The weapon that killed Janet West was there too.'

A bloodstained scaffolding pole had been pushed in beside the body. As Philip Richmond had a cord round his neck and his head was undamaged, Millson was certain the pole had been used to kill Janet. Why else hide it?

'Lowery used to be a welder and he thought of a very clever way to hide Richmond's body. Janet must have run into him with the body on her way to her appointment with Goodman. Lowery killed her, but didn't dump her body on the riverbank until much later, after he'd welded up Richmond. That's why Goodman didn't pass her body on his way home. That's what I believe happened, except that Lowery couldn't have done all that in the hour and a half he was out of the pub in Findlesham. It's an hour's drive from there to the shipyard.'

'Ah, but he could,' Scobie said jubilantly. 'He brought Richmond's body across the river by boat. It only takes five minutes by water. I've just done it in Lowery's own dory.'

Millson's face broke into a smile. 'You've cracked it, Norris! Well done!'

'Thanks, George,' Scobie said. 'But how did Pearson get hold of Janet's diary?'

'My guess is that he ran and picked it up while the fisherman who found her was in the yard phoning. He'd know he was named in it. And then he kept it to use for blackmail.'

'And his suicide?'

'Oh, I don't think he killed himself,' Millson said. 'I think Lowery killed him. Pearson probably boasted of making Janet call on him every time she had an appointment with Goodman and Lowery saw the chance to saddle him with her murder. It'd be difficult to prove, though.'

At the buffet lunch in her office, Nicola was chatting to the Wadhams. Andrew Hartman stood by the door awaiting the opportunity to speak to her and Melissa Richmond was in animated discussion with the three shareholders beneath the portrait of Bertram Richmond.

Over Elsie Wadham's shoulder, Nicola saw Chief Inspector Millson enter the room accompanied by Sergeant Scobie and a policewoman. She excused herself from the Wadhams and went to greet them.

'You look terribly stern, Chief Inspector.' She noticed the sombre look on Scobie's face. 'What's the matter? What is it?'

Millson said gravely, 'I'm afraid I have some very bad news for you, Miss Richmond. Your father has been murdered. I'm so very sorry.'

Nicola gasped and began to sway. Scobie stepped forward. So did Andrew Hartman. Nicola looked from one to the other. Suddenly, she flung herself at Andrew Hartman and buried her face in his shoulder.

Millson strode across the room, followed by the policewoman. 'Melissa Richmond, I arrest you on suspicion of the murder of your husband, Philip Richmond. You are not obliged to say anything and anything you do say . . .' A cry of anguish from Nicola drowned the rest of his caution.

As the policewoman led Melissa Richmond away, two uniformed policemen in the shipyard below threaded their way through the dispersing crowd and closed in on Thomas Lowery.

Millson rejoined a bemused Scobie. Nicola Richmond was clinging to Hartman, quietly sobbing.

Millson said in a low voice, 'She needed a daddy, Norris. A father-figure. Strong and powerful like her grandad. You weren't the type. Come on, let's go.'

Behind them as they left, Nicola said miserably, 'I've lost my father . . . I'm going to lose the yard . . . all those men will lose their jobs . . . I've failed.'

Andrew Hartman put a hand under her chin and lifted her face. 'You haven't failed, you've just changed direction. I'm going to incorporate a boatyard in the development plan. You can retrain the workforce and build steel yachts—big racing yachts.'

She looked up at him and frowned. 'Why should you do that?'

'Makes commercial sense,' he said. 'It's an expanding market.' The eyes gazing into hers conveyed another reason, though.

At home that evening George Millson told his daughter, 'Go and change. I'm taking you out for a meal.'

'What's wrong with what I've got on?' she asked suspiciously.

He eyed the faded denims and grubby T-shirt. 'You wanted me to look my best when I gave press interviews,' he said mildly. 'Perhaps you could do the same for me.'

Her face cleared. 'OK. I'll put on my new dress.' The suspicious look reappeared. 'What's this *for*?'

'Do I need a reason to take you out?'

'No-o. Not if that's all there is to it.'

'What do you mean?'

'You might be softening me up for another visit to Mum.'

George Millson drew her to him and kissed her forehead. 'You'd make a rotten detective,' he said. 'Now go and make yourself look pretty.'

Laura Stebbing visited her husband just once while he was on remand. To tell him she was leaving him. Then she moved her belongings to her friend Janet's house and went off on holiday to plan a new life for herself.